Tommie... Always finding silver linings. Seeing the good. Raising him up when he was down, filling his well. She was his silver lining for sure, shining now, blinding him, tying his heart to the train tracks.

"You're something else, you know that?"

Her gaze flickered. "Am I forgiven, though?"

"Oh, Tom..." Way to slay him, finish him off. And maybe it was blowing his cover, but right now, he couldn't make himself care. He freed his hand from hers, put it to her cheek. "Yes. A million times over."

Tears rose in her eyes. "That's a lot of times."

But she was smiling, leaning her soft, perfect cheek into his touch, and she wouldn't be doing that if she didn't *like* his touch, would she? Wouldn't be looking at him like this with that warm glow in her gaze if she didn't want...

His heart pulsed. "Oh God, Tommie..." And then, somehow, he was moving in, taking her mouth, kissing her, and she was kissing him back, her lips warm and perfect, molding to his as if they'd been designed for him.

Dear Reader,

Hello, and welcome to my tenth (how did that happen?) title for Harlequin Romance!

I have to admit—I'm not completely sure where the idea for this story came from. It was probably some television drama or movie I watched that featured a driver character, or a limo. The main thing is that the idea stuck, got me thinking about how many boxes a personal driver–client situation could tick for a heartfelt and emotional romance...

Forced proximity—tick.

Employee-boss—tick.

Beautiful heroine driver (whose real ambition is to become a top fashion designer)—tick.

Grumpy, hot billionaire hero (who counts motor racing among his many bowstrings)—tick-a-doodle-do!

Add a glamorous London setting, a secret New York connection, a raft of his-and-hers "issues," some social status disparity and a day at the motor-racing circuit, and there's a potent cocktail...

That was my thinking, anyway. Hopefully Max and Tommie's romance ticks all the right boxes for you, dear reader, and you enjoy their rocky road to happy-ever-after.

Much love,

Ella x

DRIVING HER IMPOSSIBLE BILLIONAIRE

ELLA HAYES

 Harlequin

ROMANCE

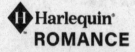

Harlequin®
ROMANCE

ISBN-13: 978-1-335-21632-8

Driving Her Impossible Billionaire

Recycling programs for this product may not exist in your area.

Harlequin Enterprises ULC
22 Adelaide St. West, 41st Floor
Toronto, Ontario M5H 4E3, Canada
www.Harlequin.com

Printed in U.S.A.

After ten years as a television camerawoman, **Ella Hayes** started her own photography business so that she could work around the demands of her young family. As an award-winning wedding photographer, she's documented hundreds of love stories in beautiful locations, both at home and abroad. She lives in central Scotland with her husband and two grown-up sons. She loves reading, traveling with her camera, running and great coffee.

Books by Ella Hayes

Harlequin Romance

Her Brooding Scottish Heir
Italian Summer with the Single Dad
Unlocking the Tycoon's Heart
Tycoon's Unexpected Caribbean Fling
The Single Dad's Christmas Proposal
Their Surprise Safari Reunion
Barcelona Fling with a Secret Prince
One Night on the French Riviera
Bound by Their Lisbon Legacy

Visit the Author Profile page at Harlequin.com.

For my dear friend Hayley, with love.

Praise for
Ella Hayes

PROLOGUE

Today's Sporting News:

*British Touring Car Championship driver
Max Lawler Scott walked away from a horrific crash at Donnington this afternoon,
clutching his left hand.*

*The thirty-three-year-old celebrity pub-
licist, who achieved a podium place four
times last year, refused to be stretchered
off, but was clearly in pain as he withdrew
from the track surrounded by officials and
medics.*

*His sister Felicity Hewitt, anchor for
News Global, later confirmed Lawler
Scott's injury to be serious, saying that
it might well preclude him from driving
again for the rest of the year. She admitted that this would be an immense blow to
the speed-loving playboy who loves to race.*

*Neither Lawler Scott's father, media
mogul Sir Gerald Scott, nor his mother,*

News Global Editor Tamsin Lawler, have made any statement, but were snapped arriving separately this evening at Cromwell Hospital, where their son is being treated...

CHAPTER ONE

Three weeks later...

'HELLO, YES? WHAT?'

Tommie felt herself flinch. Hardly the warmest of welcomes. Three words, not even polite ones, barked over the intercom! The man sounded impatient, irritated, as if she was interrupting something—but that couldn't be right because this was definitely the correct address, the correct day, and she was bang on time.

Breathe...

Maybe there was a simple explanation. Maybe this wasn't *the* person, but some poor, hard-pressed minion, who didn't know she had an actual appointment—in which case all she had to do was set him straight...

She aimed a smile into the security camera, making sure to keep her gaze and tone level. 'I'm here for the interview.' And in case that wasn't enough information... 'I'm Tommie Seager.'

Short pause.

'Tommie…?

Oh. *Of course*. Here it was. The familiar note of surprise. Next would come the half-beat of re-calibration while assumptions were laid to rest. Her sister Billie got it all the time too.

She widened her smile a touch. 'Yes, that's right.'

'Ah…'

Slithering off his high horse now, wasn't he? Regrouping. It was hard not to smirk, not to show just a touch of enjoyment, but it wouldn't endear her to him any—which was, after all, the whole point of coming. To make a good impression. Never mind that Prince not-so-Charming didn't seem to be similarly motivated. Still, if he was *the* person—the prospective employer—she didn't have to like him to work for him.

The intercom emitted a cough, then a little throat-clearing noise. 'Apologies, Tommie. I was…'

She held her breath. How could he be strug-gling when the words were so obvious? Curt. Gruff. Rude. Any of them would do.

'…distracted.'

Slippery, much?

And then his tone steadied, seeming to find its groove, public-school-polite, formal. 'Please, come in.'

A buzzer sounded, then a lock sprang in the high black gate.

She pulled in a slow breath and pushed it open.

Wow! The house was impressive. Architect-designed. Vast, but not cold, not austere. Rather, it was warmly appealing. Acres of plate glass and external lighting. A flat roof covered its two storeys, overhanging the walls by a deep margin. The walls themselves were of a polished light grey block, softened in places with narrow vertical strips of golden cedar cladding—like barcodes. The whole thing was softened further by lush, exotic planting around the perimeter and around the edges of the pale monobloc frontage. It was all very Zen. Neat. Private.

Beautiful!

She felt her eyes going to the four—yes, *four*—garage doors. What was behind them? A sleek, gull-winged sports car? Some high-end electric fantasy? Or something classic and sedate? Probably all of the above. And none of the usual garage junk. No rusty barbecue on wheels, no rolls of old carpet that 'might come in handy one day'. No way—not in a pristine place like this.

She checked herself. Now who was the one making assumptions?

She shut the gate and set off towards the front door—all charcoal-grey and brushed steel—

trying to ignore the butterflies in her stomach. Hard not to conjecture, though, when you had no actual information. That was the thing about the agency Billie worked for—Neville Cutter Services, recruitment for the rich and famous—it was all so discreet, so cloak and dagger. She'd had to sign a non-disclosure agreement just to come for this interview, and even Billie didn't know who the employer was, because names were never supplied until a candidate was accepted for a role, only details of the post being offered.

In this case, *Personal driver. Eight-month contract. Live-in. Luxury annexe accommodation.* Stapled to a *Strictly no guests, day or night* stipulation. Free run of the owner's pool and gym—although since 'erratic, unsociable hours' were promised, even at weekends, it was probably a token gesture. Days off were to be allocated on an ad hoc basis to fit with the employer's schedule. It was basically twenty-four-seven, which was why the job paid a fortune—a fortune that could change Tommie's life. *That* was why Billie had called her the moment it had landed on Neville's desk.

'It's got your name all over it, Tommie! You've got the skills. The experience. And I know you're going to say you don't want to go back to driving, but think of the money and the free

*accommodation—in Hampstead, no less. No
more living with Mum and Dad! And I get that
it's demanding, but it's only eight months, and
then you'd have the funds you need to go for it.
And, yes, there's all that waiting around—but,
hey...old news, right? And I'm not trying to wind
you up about New York, because I know you're
still livid, but you learned a lot too—so why not
use it? Use the waiting around time to sketch,
develop some new ideas, make overtures to buyers. I mean the Lincoln Lawyer worked out of
his car, so why not you, Tommie? Why not you?'*

Launching her own fashion label from the
front seat of some billionaire's luxury ride
seemed a tad far-fetched—but, oh, the money...
the possibilities it could deliver. As for the annexe accommodation... A place of her very own
for the first time in her life. Never mind that it
would only be for eight months, at least for those
eight months it would be hers—all of it. A place
to be herself, to breathe, think, sketch, dream...
No Mum and Dad, no New York roomies, no
Jamie...

She felt her chest tightening on cue. Ridiculous to *still* be feeling guilty about Jamie. It
wasn't as if any of what happened was by design. She hadn't *asked* him to chat her up in the
pub that night...hadn't *asked* him to ask her out,

or to offer her a job three months later, driving for his family's start-up business Chauffeur Me.

She hadn't asked, but of course chauffeuring was a step up from delivery driving—more glamorous, better paid—so of course she'd accepted. Who in their right mind wouldn't have? But she'd never asked to become so involved in the business, to get caught up in the constant in-fighting—Jamie and his dad; his dad and his brother—had never asked to become chief mediator or to become the driver most favoured by their female celebrity clients, the one businesswomen felt most comfortable with. She'd never asked for those five years to slip by in a blur, never asked Jamie to propose. And she totally should have but never had asked herself why she'd said yes, moved in with him.

It had all been slow drifting—until it hadn't. Until the day she'd got the gig driving iconic fashion designer Chloe Mills for the whole of London Fashion Week. A glorious week! Talking non-stop fashion with Chloe, feeling the old fires stirring, brightening inside, confessing to Chloe-freaking-Mills, of all people, that she designed stuff too—had used to do Spitalfields Market with a friend every Saturday, selling her own creations.

Used to… Because she didn't any more.

Didn't have the time, or the focus, because of

Jamie and *his* business…because she'd somehow let her dreams drift away.

It had been a sobering behind-the-wheel re-alisation—one that would have been bound to change things anyway. But that last morning she hadn't asked Chloe to offer her a dream job, to be her personal assistant in New York, and she hadn't asked to be faced with making that decision in that moment.

Chloe had asked *her*. And how could she have turned it down, the chance of lifetime, when mostly life had dealt her short straws?

Yes, it had meant blindsiding Jamie, hurting him, leaving him a driver short. And, no, it hadn't been her finest hour. But she hadn't planned it—any of it. Still, Jamie could content himself with the last laugh, because here she was eighteen months later, back in London with her tail between her legs, shafted, and smarting.

So much for once-in-a-lifetime chances, so-called golden opportunities!

She shook herself. But now wasn't the time to be dissing golden opportunities—not when she was staring down the barrel of another one, and not when Billie had pushed her to the top of Neville's pile to give her the jump on the other candidates. She owed it her best shot—owed Billie. And maybe chauffeuring again did feel like a backward step, but at least this time it was a means to an end. And it was infinitely better than tidying the ravaged clothes rails at Belle & Trend, for little more than minimum wage, kidding herself that she was still working in fashion.

Bottom line: Billie was right. This job had her name all over it. All she had to do was win over Mr Grumpy!

She squared herself up to the door, lifting her hand, but before she could bring it down to knock the door was opening wide, revealing a tall, fair, sickeningly familiar figure.

'Tommie?' Laser-blue eyes swept over her without a vestige of recognition, and then he broke into a slightly forced-looking smile, extending his hand for her to shake. 'Max Scott. Thanks for coming.'

She felt dryness seizing her throat, her heart seizing altogether. *No, no, no!* This could *not* be happening. Max Scott! Well, he could call himself that if he liked, but it didn't alter the fact that this was *the* Maxwell Lawler Scott, publicist to the rich and shady. Worse, he was Chloe Mills' publicist—lying, thieving Chloe Mills, who'd stolen her designs and passed them off as her own, then fired her when she'd got up the nerve to challenge her about it. Not that he was likely to know about that, since Chloe would hardly have confessed it to her publicist, of all people, but, still, he was on Chloe's team, and as such the enemy.

She found a steadying patch of breath. At least he didn't seem to recognise her. Then again, why would he? Thanks to Billie, there was nothing in her application to jog his memory. No mention of New York, no mention of her working for Chloe. Billie had said they should leave it out because it was irrelevant, and it might actually count against her—make her seem like not a serious enough candidate for a personal driver position. And it wasn't as if he'd given her more than a passing glance that long-ago night when she'd run into him—*literally*—back in her early days of working for Chloe, back when it had all still felt so exciting…

New York Fashion Week… Chloe's after-show party…

Chloe had sent her scurrying to organise more canapés, because they were going to run short. She'd said it to her in that arch way she had, implying it was *her* fault—which it absolutely hadn't been. But, as she'd quickly learned, Chloe was a highly strung control freak who insisted on signing off on everything from buttons and fabric swatches to the exact number of freaking canapés.

She'd been flying out through the door as Max had been coming in, with supermodel Saskia

Riva on his arm. She'd caught him with her shoulder momentarily, and nearly died on the spot because he was so utterly drop-dead gorgeous. But before she'd been able to stammer out an apology he'd swept on as if he hadn't felt the impact—as if she'd made no impact on him at all.

And now here he was, looking at her with a perplexed and visibly narrowing gaze. Narrowing because she was still silent, rooted to the spot, instead of greeting him back, shaking his hand like a normal person, falling over herself to make a good impression.

Well, that boat had clearly sailed. His expression spoke volumes. He wasn't going to employ her, was probably wondering why the agency had sent her at all.

Her heart lurched. *Oh, God!* And that wasn't going to reflect well on the agency or on Billie, was it?

For Billie's sake—even though this was suddenly the last job in the world she wanted—she needed to step up, show Max she was a contender, not a complete waste of his time.

Breathe, Tommie.

'Max...' She put her hand into his, shaking firmly to seem confident. 'Thanks for seeing me.' *And now smile...* 'It's very nice to meet you.'

He gave a slow nod, his lips parting slightly as

if he wasn't sure what to say, and then he seemed to rally, stepping aside with a new, tight smile. 'Please, come in.'

She forced her feet to move, but a few steps in they were faltering again, along with her breath.

It was so light inside…so airy, calm and serene. Unexpected, somehow, for a renowned man about town. *A player!* She pushed the thought away. Maybe all the plants had something to do with it—large, expensive specimens, lush and green and not remotely dying, like her plants always were. Or maybe it was the acres of solid Maplewood flooring, the pale couches, and all the lovely natural textures that made the place feel so tranquil and homely…those warm accents of red earth and charcoal-black.

A soft *thunk* filled the silence. Max closing the door.

'Come on through.'

And then he was skimming past, trailing a pleasant soapy smell, leading the way towards the rear of the house, where vast windows were pulled back, letting in the balmy morning air and the dappled green of the garden beyond.

She felt her lungs releasing. Here was a second to breathe, to take him in. Dark blond hair, curling at his nape, nice shoulders…broad, muscular, shifting smoothly as he walked. He was wearing a plain black tee shirt, loose black trackies and…

she heard the quiet catch of her own breath...
some kind of splint on his left hand.

She stared at it. So that was why he needed
a driver—and why he was dressed like that.
Pull-on, pull-off stuff was probably the best he
could manage with one hand. Her heart pinched.
It must be awkward as hell. And this was an
eight-month contract, wasn't it? So he would be
anticipating eight months of awkwardness. No
wonder he wasn't exactly radiating sunshine.
She wouldn't be either, in his shoes. Not that
she could let herself feel sorry for him. She had
one job: to spend five minutes presenting herself
well, so that Billie wouldn't seem incompetent,
and then she was out of here!

CHAPTER TWO

SHE WAS LOOKING him over. He could tell. He could feel her grey-green eyes burning into his back, drilling holes into his skull... Or maybe that was just a tension headache coming on, because, God help him, she was even more attractive in the flesh than she'd looked on the Entryphone camera. Heart-shaped face. Milky complexion. Sweet full lips reddened with confident lipstick. Impeccable, too. Professional-looking, with her efficient blonde chignon and her crisp white shirt. Her pale grey suit was well cut, the trousers fashionably cropped above pristine black patent loafers. She was dream stuff—if you were into those sorts of dreams—quite the package!

But what was with the attitude? That cool, vaguely baiting gaze she'd greeted him with before she'd so obviously reminded herself that she ought to smile. It wasn't the puzzled flash of half recognition he sometimes got from strangers; it was something else. Almost as if he'd offended her in some way. But how? He'd only known her for two minutes and barely opened his mouth in that time.

Unless...

He raked his teeth over his lip. Unless it was because he'd been a tad irritable over the intercom. Initially, anyway. Not his fault! How was he to have known she was the candidate? He'd thought she was trying to sell him something: encyclopaedias...gym membership. *Whatever!* Taking up his time when he was expecting a guy to pitch up for an interview any second.

Honest mistake!

No, Max. Not remotely honest...

Felicity's voice, in his head, reprimanding him as only a sister could. He ground his jaw. She was right, of course—as always. If he'd taken the time to read Tommie's details properly, instead of skimming them literally as the buzzer was sounding, he'd have known she was female. But no. Too busy fuming about this whole intolerable situation to spend five minutes preparing—fuming because he didn't want anyone living here—even in the guest annexe—invading his sanctuary, seeing him reduced like this, fencing with this useless hand.

He focused hard, trying to detect some sensation, but it was no good. He couldn't make his fingers feel...move. Didn't stop him trying, though, did it? Constantly. Involuntarily. Like a dog with bone. Trying to force feeling through wrecked nerves that might or might not knit themselves back together in the correct register. Months of uncertainty lay ahead, with no guarantee of being able to grip again, pick up a cup, drive—race!

And maybe Fliss was right. Maybe he *was* taking the specialist's direst warnings too much to heart instead of embracing the rosier picture, that he *might* get most of the function back, and the feeling. But he didn't want to feed his hopes only to have them dashed. Bad enough listening to the preachy voice inside his head saying he only had himself to blame, because he was the one who'd put himself in that car, on that track.

He knew the risks…took the risks. For heaven's sake, he knew accidents happened!

He pulled his lips tight. He'd just never thought that one would happen to him. Not deep down. Too welded to the myth of his own invincibility, too hooked on racing. On the strategy, the split-second decisions, the pure adrenaline rush of it. But he wasn't invincible. And now, because he wasn't, he needed a driver, must tolerate a stranger living in his personal space because he couldn't—just couldn't—spend the foreseeable future waiting for cabs to come, relinquishing his independence on top of everything else.

And not only because his clients paid him a lot of money to be available round the clock, but because freedom was the air he breathed—*must* breathe.

A trade-off, then. Necessary. But he hadn't expected, wasn't prepared for Tommie Seager. Cool. Unfathomable. Threatening to send his brains south even while she was for some inexplicable reason totally freaking him out. No way could he employ her, cope with this kind of discombobulation on a daily basis. This whole thing was a bust—a waste of time. But he was stuck now…must force himself to go through the motions, at least give her the interview she'd come for.

He made for the kitchen end of the living area, then drew in a breath and turned to face her. 'I thought we could chat in here…'

Because the centre island was two and a half metres wide—the perfect amount of distance to put between them.

He motioned for her to sit. 'Can I get you something? Tea? Coffee?'

She flicked a glance at his injured hand. 'No, just water, thanks.' And then her gaze came to his, opening out a little. 'If you tell me where the glasses are, I'll get it myself…'

He felt his chest tighten. She was being considerate. But he didn't want consideration. It only made things worse, amplified his frustration, that feeling burning inside him that he wasn't fully in control any more.

He forced out a smile. 'Thanks, but it's fine. I'll get it...'

He crossed to the cupboard where he kept the glasses and took one down. Easy enough to pop it into the fridge door water dispenser and pull the lever. As for himself, he'd have coffee—not because he really wanted one, but because he wanted her to see that he could set a cup into the machine, slap in a pod and set it going. Maybe it was petty...petulant of him...but he couldn't help it. He was frustrated on more levels than he could count, and if showing her that he was perfectly capable of rustling up two simple beverages soothed something inside him then why not do it?

She was watching, at least. He could feel the weight of her gaze on his back, feel it siphoning the strength from his legs. But then suddenly the weight was lightening, lifting away.

'You have a lovely home, Max.'

He felt a small, reluctant swell of warmth. Did she mean it or was she just making small talk? Who knew? And what did it matter? The only thing that mattered was that *he* liked his home. He'd put a lot of time and thought into the design of the place, the décor and the landscaping, all to get it just so. If she genuinely liked it—great. If not—also great. But for politeness' sake he ought to say something…acknowledge the compliment.

He mustered a suitably appreciative tone. 'Thanks.'

'Have you lived here long?'

'About five years…'

He reached to extract his steaming cup from the coffee machine, felt his breath check. *Idiot!* He hadn't thought this through, had he? Two drinks meant making two separate trips—one to deliver her water and one to fetch his own coffee. He sank his teeth into his lip so hard it hurt. So much for showing her how capable he was! The only thing she was going to see now was how utterly useless—

'And do you live alone?'

What? Why was she asking him that? What did his relationship status have to do with anything? And if he told her, disclosed that he was single, would she ply him with further impertinent questions, like *Why?* Christ, as if he had the time or the remotest inclination to get into that…divulge the details of his difficult journey to this blissful state of total self-reliance—*control*—where no one could touch him, sideline him, make him feel *less*.

And maybe Fliss was right—he *was* too sen-

sitive, had taken everything too hard growing up, building a wall around himself because
of it. But what was wrong with that if he was
happy? He didn't diss *her* choices, did he? He
was pleased that she was all loved up with her
husband Gavin, joyfully newly pregnant. But he
didn't want what she wanted—wasn't up for pin-
ning his whole happiness on someone else, giving someone else that power over him. He was
fine as he was, wasn't up for having his hard-
won equilibrium wrecked by heartbreak.

Because that was what always happened in
the end. He'd seen it too many times, spent too
many years papering over ugliness for his clients, managing the media around their various
heartbreaks, infidelities or plain old foolish in-
discretions, to believe that love was real, something meant to last.

The fact was, all relationships were trans-
actional—whether the people in them realised
it or not. Ultimately everyone was out to get
something from the other person. Money. Status. Power. Advancement. Certainly the women
who hit on him always seemed to have one eye
trained on what he could do for them. And, yes,
maybe that was a hazard of the job, down to the
circles he moved in, but it didn't exactly swell
the heart, make it skip.

So, no, he wasn't diving into that shark tank,

and if by staying out of it he'd earned himself a playboy reputation, then so what? It wasn't true, but it suited his purposes…ensured that the women who approached him were primed not to expect romance or commitment. As if he had time for any of that anyway. Lawler Scott PR kept him busy enough—and now he had his brand-new venture to handle as well: motor sports news agency Alpha News. And of course motor racing was king—the absolute love of his life.

He frowned down at the still-steaming coffee cup. It was a good life, all in all. One he liked…enjoyed. He was happy running along in his groove. He liked his house, his own space, his own company—and privacy. *Especially* privacy. So whatever Tommie was angling for with her question, the only thing she was going to catch was a cold!

He drew in a breath and turned. 'I…'

But the rest wouldn't come. Because for some reason—*why?*—she was on her feet, gliding through the precious buffer zone towards him, foxing him with her perfume and her level grey-green gaze. He could feel his jaw trying to slacken, and a very inconvenient stirring sensation happening down below—which, in these track pants, might draw her attention if he didn't do something about it and fast!

He made a quick pivot, pulling out a drawer to cover himself, rooting for a spoon he didn't need. 'I do live alone, yes.'

'Ah...' She came to a graceful stop by the fridge, carefully removing the glass of water from its little shelf in the door—seemingly the thoughtful point of her mission—and then her eyes came to his, her gaze dispassionate. 'I wasn't prying...' She adjusted her grip on her glass. 'I was only asking because it must be tricky not having anyone around to help you with your hand like that...'

He felt his heart skidding off its rails. Well, wasn't she the candid one? It was refreshing—sort of. But still, he wasn't getting into this with her. All the different ways life had become tricky, the coping strategies he'd had to devise just to get by these past three weeks, such as living in pull-on clothes. No doubt she'd noticed his uber-casual attire, given that she'd put herself together so well...

For an interview. Which he was somehow, very successfully, failing to give her.

Focus, Max!

'I manage.' He set the spoon down and picked up his cup, seizing the moment. 'Shall we sit?'

She obliged, going back to her spot, positioning her glass in front of her. He parked his coffee, then himself, trying to recall what he'd read about her.

'So, you've worked as a chauffeur before?'

'Yes.' She nodded slightly. 'I was with Chauffeur Me for five years.'

A familiar crowd, highly reputable—not that he'd ever used them.

'And you enjoyed it?' Pointless question, but it sounded good…made him feel as if he was controlling the show.

'Yes.' She nodded again, then smiled as if she thought she should. 'I liked meeting different people. And it was more interesting than delivery driving.'

'Which is what you did before you became a chauffeur?'

'Yes, for three years.' A different smile touched her lips, some private amusement. 'I did like driving vans, though.'

He tried to picture her behind the wheel of some great high-top thing, screeching up to his door, swinging out with a parcel and a scanner device…

'What did you like about it?'

Her mouth straightened. 'I liked that it gave me an encyclopaedic knowledge of London, and I liked the challenge of driving a van… Working around the limited visibility, reverse parking into tight spots and so on. It taught me how to use my mirrors well, to know my blind spots.' Her eyebrows lifted a little. 'It made me a better driver.'

Textbook answers, designed to impress. Unlike himself, she'd obviously prepared for this interview, knew which boxes to tick.

'So, I assume you've got a clean licence?'

Her gaze flared an incredulous degree. 'Of course.'

Nice one, Max!

Because he'd stipulated an unblemished licence, hadn't he? Or rather, his sister had. Fliss was the one who'd helped him get his act together with this whole hiring a driver thing, so he could 'get on with living' while his hand got on with healing. If only she'd agreed to help him with the interviewing as well, but when he'd asked her she'd just stared at him.

'It's a driver, Max! How hard can it be?'

Quite hard, as it was turning out. Because Tommie wasn't 'Tommy'. And maybe it was wrong to view her differently because she wasn't a guy, but he couldn't help it. She was beautiful, and beneath that cool, composed exterior there was clearly a warm heart beating—a kind heart—offering to get her own glass of water like that, then collecting it for herself, subtly saving him from his pathetic, self-inflicted quandary. Impossible to imagine that a girl like this didn't have a life to be living. Friends. *A lover*...

And, no, it wasn't any of his business—except that he couldn't consider anyone, male or female, who wasn't free to be at his absolute beck and call. Not that he *was* actually considering her, but if he didn't interview her thoroughly as if he were she'd no doubt suss him out for a fake. So he had to continue, ask her the questions the way he'd ask anyone...

He took a sip of his coffee and met her gaze. 'So, how do you feel about the demands of the position?'

Her brow wrinkled. 'Which particular demands?'

'The hours. The living arrangements.' His temples pulsed. 'The rules...'

She pursed her lips. 'I'm fine with all of it.'

Or was she just saying she was? Filling his ears with the music she thought he wanted to hear in order to seem like a good candidate, to win him over? No chance of that. But still, to make the charade seem real he couldn't not dig deeper.

'You're fine with having to be here unless I give you leave?'

'Yes.'

'Fine with not having any guests over? Day or night. Family. Friends...' He could feel his pores starting to prickle, his headache striking up again. But he had to say it. '*Special* friends.'

Her eyebrows lifted. 'Are you trying to ask me if I *have* a special friend?'

That frankness again, stripping him for parts. But it was fine; he could be just as frank.

'No, I'm not.' And just in case she was reading between non-existent lines… 'It's of no personal interest to me whatsoever. I'm simply trying to make my position clear. I'm paying a lot for a driver because I realise I'm asking a lot. And I'm asking a lot because I'm a very private person…'

Weird and slightly obsessive, Fliss would say. But if admitting it was what it took to clarify things, then so be it.

He drew in a breath. 'I have a thing about personal space, okay?'

Something dislodged in her gaze. 'I can relate to that…'

So he wasn't the only one. He felt a valve releasing somewhere. If she got it, then he could just say it, couldn't he? Not sugarcoat it.

He looked at her. 'Truth is, I don't want anyone living here at all. But circumstances have dictated otherwise, so here we are. I need to find the right person—someone I can see fitting in. And I need that person to stay…not be drawn away by personal issues or obligations.

I don't want to be going through all this hiring business again.'

She nodded. 'I understand....' She looked down, toying with her glass for a moment and then her gaze lifted, clear, and direct. 'I don't have any obligations, personal or otherwise. My family lives in London, so if you were to offer me this position I could see them even if I only had an hour or two off. But in any case they'd know the demands of the job, so...' She gave a little a shrug and then, for an instant, her gaze opened like a window. 'I'm living at home with my parents at the moment so, as you can imagine, the live-in aspect is a quite a draw.'

Living with her parents...

Why would she be living with her parents at— what? Twenty-eight, twenty-nine years old? He felt his eyes staring into hers...searching. Was it the same reason she was free of obligations, why she didn't have a *special* friend? Not that she'd exactly answered that question. More deflected it. But it all pointed to a break-up of some sort—some big life-change which made her one hundred percent available, one hundred percent unlikely to leave him in the lurch. In short, it made her even more perfect for the position than she was already.

He felt a tide rising, crashing over him. Damn this interview! He'd meant it to be a token gesture—a quick formality before he showed her the door. But here he was, still sitting in front of her, and there she was, looking at him with that gaze of hers, somehow changing every dimension in the room and any second now she was going to notice that he was losing control of this thing…floundering. He had to shake himself, say something quickly—anything to bring this to a close.

'So…' He picked up his cup to buy a moment, and then he had it—the perfect interview-like thing to say. He allowed himself a quick sip and the briefest of smiles. 'I think I've got everything I need. Do you have anything you'd like to ask me?'

This would be the moment to get up and smile, say, *No, I'm good, thanks,* then leave. So why wasn't she doing that?

Why?

She swallowed hard. God knew. But for some infuriating reason she couldn't seem make herself move, couldn't free herself from that compelling blue gaze. And at any moment those eyes were going to narrow, and those dark straight brows were going draw in, and those beautiful lips were going to part slightly—because she was sitting here silent. So she had to think of something fast—*anything!*

And then it was there, staring her in the face. The obvious question...the one that had been burning her candle at both ends from the moment she'd noticed his splint.

'Yes, I do actually...' She pulled in a breath. 'What did you do to your hand?'

His brows lifted. 'My hand?'

He seemed taken aback, but it was a reasonable enough question. His injury was the reason he needed a driver. And it was obviously troubling him...hampering him physically, mentally, giving his pride a workout. *Geez!* Such a performance with the drinks...getting himself in a tuck—and all for what? To show her he was Cool Hand Luke, able to triumph in the face of adversity? It had been hard not to laugh, watching him, but at the same time impossible not to feel for him, so she'd had to get up and help. And he hadn't said anything, but he'd noticed, all right. Because there'd been a sweet moment of gratitude in his eyes...

Was that why she was still sitting here? Because that glimmer he'd shown her—that peek behind the mask—was tugging at all the usual strings, appealing to the good nature she'd been saddled with. That impulse she had to look for the best in people, to care about them...help them? If so, then she was crazy, and she needed to stop right now. Because that impulse always backfired so that *she* lost out...

Jamie. His dream. His business. His family. Squeezing her dreams out of the picture.

Then Chloe. Trying to help her when she had been blocked creatively. Talking inspiration with her...concepts. Showing her some of her own work, thinking it might refresh Chloe's and, yes, maybe hoping to impress her too. Hoping that Chloe might give her a chance, as she'd promised to do, a tiny slot in a show...at the front... at the end. Just a moment in the spotlight to set her dreams free... Tommie Seager Designs...

She felt her stomach hardening. Well, she'd got a spot in the show, all right. Her designs. Choe's name. No comeback. Just a shove out through the door and a ticket home.

She drew Max back into focus. And here he was. Chloe's publicist—*Chloe's guy.* Appealing as hell with his wounded blue eyes and tousled hair, appealing as hell despite his uptight demeanour and silly, masculine pride. But she couldn't let her caring nature win, let him think she was asking for any other reason than to establish how his injury might impact the business of working for him.

Should that situation arise.

She nodded, trying to keep her gaze level, trying not to hate herself for being so matter of fact. 'Yes, your hand… I mean, that's why I'm here, isn't it?'

He blinked. 'Indeed.' And then he set his cup down. 'I was in a car crash.'

'Oh, my God! Where?' As if *that* mattered. But it was out of her mouth now, attached to an all too obvious note of horrified concern.

'Donnington.'

The word spun for a beat.

'You mean, the racetrack…?'

'Yes.'

Racing one of those lovelies sequestered in the four-door garage, no doubt.

'Track day?'

He shook his head. 'No. I was racing.'

She felt her breath pause, her eyes staring into his. But he wasn't a racing driver. He was a PR guy! International city slicker, celebrity apologist, chisel-jawed escort to supermodels. Sharp-suited, sharp-witted all-round mover, shaker and schmoozer. He *wasn't* a racing driver!

Except… His gaze was serious, deadly deep, reaching in all the way to her toes, which was a very unnerving sensation.

She swallowed hard. 'You're saying you're a racing driver?'

'Not exclusively—but, yes. I race touring cars.'

'Like…saloon cars?'

He made a little impatient noise. 'Modified, race-prepared touring cars. They look like regular cars on the outside, but that's where the similarity ends.'

She bit down hard on her lip. But it was no good—she couldn't *not* ask, couldn't make herself *not* want to know. 'So, what happened?'

A shadow flitted through his gaze. 'My car was clipped by another driver at one hundred and twelve miles per hour. It flipped and rolled, and now my left hand is wrecked.'

She felt her eyes going to his splint, her traitorous heart squeezing. *What to say?* Pointless telling him he was lucky to be alive. He knew that—must have heard it a hundred times already. What was plaguing him now, moving behind his eyes, was *how* wrecked his hand was… the extent of it. And she didn't want to rub salt into his wound, even though he was the enemy, but she wanted to know—couldn't stop herself from wanting to…

'I'm sorry, Max.' She took a breath. 'What's the prognosis?'

His eyebrows flickered. 'You don't hold back, do you?'

But maybe he didn't mind. His gaze wasn't abrasive…wasn't making her think she couldn't come back at him.

'It's a natural question. You just told me your

hand is wrecked. Am I supposed to ignore it… sit here silent? I think you'd think I was odd if I did.'

His eyes registered the logic, the light inside them softening momentarily. 'You have a point.' But then his features were tightening again. 'The prognosis is currently uncertain. The bones will mend, but there's some nerve damage.' He threw a disparaging glance at the offending hand. 'I can't feel anything, don't know when, or if, I ever will again.'

She felt an echo inside…recognition stirring. She knew that anxious state-of-limbo feeling. Not that it was the same, or even came close, but when she was fifteen she'd somehow contracted glandular fever. It had floored her—dragged on for weeks before her mock exams. She'd thought she would never come right again. Turned out, she'd been right. Because she never had come right…hadn't seemed to settle back into school afterwards, hadn't been able to get to grips with the work she'd missed. She'd flunked her big summer exams and kept on going, spiralling downwards.

That was until the day she'd passed her driving test. Everything had changed then. Driving had saved her—opened the world up again. Driving those vans, tearing around all day long delivering stuff, had made her feel she *was* somebody. Worthy. In control of her life. Powerful…

She looked at Max. Staring down at his cup now, his face drawn. Had he felt powerful before the crash? In control? And now fate had flipped his coin and he was having to hand control to someone else just to get about…losing his independence, his precious privacy. For a man like him, who oozed privilege from every single one of his beautiful pores—a man who'd probably never suffered a single setback in his whole charmed life—it must be devastating.

She couldn't let herself feel too sorry for him, though. He could afford the best care, the best surgeons and physios. It was grim, for sure, but not as grim as it would have been for someone ordinary like her. Still, she didn't want to seem heartless…couldn't leave without trying to gee him up a bit first.

She took a quick sip from her glass and set it down. 'I don't know anything about these things, but there must be some hope, surely?'

He drew in a breath that sounded like a sigh in the making. 'There is, but I don't want to cling to it. I need to be realistic.'

'I get that—as long as you don't let *realistic* become pessimistic.'

His eyes flashed. 'You sound like my sister.'

Which was what? A good thing or a bad thing?
Fifty-fifty.

She drew in a breath. 'Well, she sounds like a sensible person to me.'

'She is. Irritatingly so.'

But his gaze was softening with affection. So he was fond of his sister…

Stick with it, Tommie.

'Does she live in London?'

He nodded.

A sister in London… It wasn't much to have in common, but still…

'Mine does too. Her name is Billie.'

'Billie?' The corner of his mouth twitched upwards. 'Did your parents want boys, by any chance?'

A barely-there smile, but nevertheless genuine. Transforming. *Attractive*… Not that she could let herself fall under its spell.

She slid her eyebrows up to put him down. 'Oddly enough, I've never heard that joke before.'

His eyes registered the sarcasm with a flicker. 'Sorry.' But then he was leaning forward a little, looking at her. 'There's got to be story behind your names, though?'

One he obviously wanted to hear. Did she want to tell it, though? All she'd been trying to do was lift his mood—not get into an actual flowing conversation. But then, she was the one who'd started the ball rolling, wasn't she? And he was responding, being different from how he'd been before, and—God help her—she could feel curiosity burning inside her to see more of this different Max and, even though curiosity had done for the cat—which, by the way, had had nine actual lives to her paltry one—she couldn't switch it off any more than she could button her lip and not answer. Because not answering him would be immature and just…weird!

She took a quick sip from her glass, trying not to look too engaged. 'It's not much of a story. My dad's a Billie Holiday fan—hence Billie. And my mum had an eccentric great-aunt called Thomasina—'

'So, you're Thomasina?'

He was twisting his mouth to one side, as if trying to stop himself from laughing, but it was good-natured, not cruel, and it was doing some-thing magical to his eyes that was infuriatingly attractive and somehow infectious.

She absorbed the giggle she could feel rising into the tightest smile she could manage. 'No. I got off lightly with a modern upgrade. I'm just Tommie.'

His mouth opened, then closed again, as if he'd thought better of saying whatever it was he'd been about to say. And then he was looking down, moving his cup aside, even though it wasn't in the way.

'So, would you like to see the accommodation before you go?'

Seriously?

Was he actually *considering* her for the position?

Because he didn't seem the type to waste his time on pointless missions like showing someone the living quarters if he didn't feel they were worth his time. The thing was, she *wasn't* worth his time. She'd only been trying to present herself well for Billie's sake, and the agency's, not for his.

She blew out a slow, quiet breath. Or maybe she was getting ahead of herself—jumping to conclusions—*assuming!* After all, he wasn't exactly meeting her eye right now, was he? Nor giving her *You're the one* vibes? In fact, truth to tell, he seemed somewhat restive, unsettled. As if...

She felt her pulse slowing. So maybe this was just a formality, then—a way of moving things along because he *wasn't* interested, was trying to bring things to a polite close.

Whatever!

Bringing this to a close was perfect. A relief! She'd already stayed longer than she'd meant to, anyway. She didn't even *need* to see the accommodation, although if it was like the rest of the house it was bound to be gorgeous…

She chewed the corner of her lip. Maybe there'd be no harm in seeing it, since he was offering. No harm in showing a bit of enthusiasm to complete the whole presenting herself well charade. For Billie's sake. Obviously.

'So…?' Max shifted his cup back the other way and looked up, his gaze firm. 'Do you want to see it?'

'Sure…' She switched on a smile. 'I'd love to.'

CHAPTER THREE

'I'M SO PLEASED you found someone, Max.' His sister's voice through the speaker was warm, relieved. 'It'll make such a difference.'

'Yes, it will…'

Although Fliss was only thinking about his independence—not the difference it would make having Tommie around twenty-four-seven. That was the difference he was wrestling with…the decision that was still blinking right or wrong inside his head, even though he'd thought long and hard before making it. Even though he'd interviewed three other candidates before reaching it. Top-notch people. Qualified. Experienced. But for some reason Tommie had stuck—wouldn't let him go—so he'd gone with her.

'So, what's he like?'

He felt himself bracing. 'Well, for a start, he's a she.'

'Oh!'

Silence. Somewhat loaded. And then…

'Okay… I'll rephrase: what's *she* like?'

'Polite, professional, experienced.'

'Attractive?'

He clenched his stomach. How did his sister always manage to do this: light on the one thing that was relevant but shouldn't be? The one thing that was gnawing him to the bone? The worry that, deep down, he'd offered Tommie the job because she was gorgeous and turned him on.

He swallowed, trying to sound nonchalant. 'She's okay.'

Fliss chuckled. 'Have you any idea how transparent you are?'

His body pulsed hot. 'And have you any idea how *annoying* you are?'

'Now, now…keep your hair on. I said you're transparent, not shallow. She obviously hits the mark professionally or the agency wouldn't have sent her. If she's attractive as well, then great!' And then suddenly there was pause, and a vague kerfuffle. 'Oh, bother! Sorry, Max. Can I put you on hold for a sec? I've got another call coming in.'

'Sure…'

Situation normal! Fliss's life at the news desk was a perpetual whirl.

He got up to make a coffee, felt his angst abating a little. Whether Fliss had meant to make it or not, she did have a point. Tommie *did* tick all the professional boxes. She *was* gorgeous, of course, and got his motor running as all gorgeous women did. *That* was just biology! Pure animal impulse. But she'd also genuinely been the best candidate, had brought that bit extra to the table.

Kindliness, for one thing. Oh, he hadn't been looking for it, didn't expect—or *want*—anyone running around after him on account of his injury. But still, none of the other three had got up to fetch their own drink as Tommie had—he'd run the same the routine with them as a test. And none of them had asked him about his hand either. Which was fine, perhaps an indicator of professional discretion and detachment—absolutely on point. And yet… Tommie's directness had felt intriguing. *Refreshing!* And then, of course, none of the other three had been anything like as enthusiastic about the annexe as Tommie…

He felt a smile coming. All that studied coolness in her had given way to what had looked like pure delight when he'd taken her up. There had been joy on her face as she'd trailed her fingers lovingly over the kitchen counters and the chair-backs, and her eyes had shone like magic in the bedroom, practically popping out of her head in the bathroom. Pandering to his pride, no doubt, because he loved his home, had put so much of himself into making it perfect. But it couldn't have all been an act to win him over, because everything he'd shown her—way more than he'd intended—had got the same sparkling reaction. The pool, the gym, the cars in the garage…all bringing a glow to her face, her eyes.

What to do? She'd left an indelible impression. He'd tried so hard to shake it off, tried so hard to make himself consider the others, but the truth was they'd never stood a chance.

His phone blared with some brief, unintelligible cacophony and then Fliss was back, her voice breathless, slightly harried.

'Max, are you there?'

He raised his own voice so it would carry. 'Yes, still here.'

'So, where was I…?'

He carried his coffee back to the island unit and sat down. 'You were saying how great it is that my new driver is attractive.'

'Ah, yes… So, I was going to add that attractive is all very well, but remember she's only a driver, Max—not to mention an employee. So don't go getting your back seat mixed up with your front seat.'

His pulse jumped. *Seriously?* Offering up *'only a driver'* before getting to the substantially more important fact of Tommie being his employee! Fliss was a diamond—his best friend in the world—but sometimes…just sometimes… she was far too much like his parents.

He wanted to scream, *Don't be such an insufferable snob!* But if he did it would only come back to bite him—make him sound as if he had actual designs on Tommie, which of course he didn't!

He squeezed his lids shut, trying to cool his veins. He would never cross the employer-employee divide. God help him, he'd crossed too many lines with Tommie already. Allowing himself to feel some warm, real curiosity about her, almost blurting out that he liked her name when she'd said that thing about how she'd got off lightly not being named Thomasina. Offering her the job when it was the total opposite of what he'd resolved to do sixty seconds into the interview!

That was more than enough line-crossing as far as Tommie was concerned. It was clean slate all the way from here on in. Professional distance! He was already striking a pure note, wasn't he? Starting as he meant to go on, keeping well away while she moved in—which she was currently doing, ably assisted by Isak, his gardener-handyman.

Not that he hadn't done his bit to make her feel welcome. He'd seen to getting her fridge and cupboards stocked with some basics from the deli, and he'd asked Jenny, his cleaner, to make up the bed and give the place a good going over, because the other three applicants had tramped their feet through it, hadn't they? And absolutely he would check in with her later, to give her tomorrow's itinerary, but he was going to keep it brief, polite and formal. So Fliss could take a great big hike with her unwanted and completely unwarranted advice!

He took a sip of coffee, permitting himself some sarcasm. 'Thanks for that, Fliss. I honestly don't know how I'd get by without you here to keep me on the straight and narrow. And, by the way, *she* has a name.'

Stunned silence, and then… 'Oh, God! I'm sorry, Max. I'm being an absolute cow.' She sighed heavily. 'It must be the pregnancy hormones.'

Which maybe it was—partly at least. His heart pinched. Poor Fliss. He'd sort of stolen her thunder by getting nailed on the track just as she and Gavin announced they were expecting. He felt a prick of guilt. He hadn't even asked her how she was feeling today, had he?

He made his voice gentle. 'Are you getting morning sickness?'

'Don't even get me started!'

He felt a smile coming. 'Okay, then you're forgiven on the grounds of being seriously knocked up. By the way, tell Gavin if he needs a refuge…'

'Oh, ha-ha, aren't you funny!' And then her

voice was filling with a smile. 'He says I look *"glowing".*'

'Well, he would say that, wouldn't he? He's probably terrified of you!'

'Oh, Lord, now you're on a roll…' She chuckled, then drew in an audible breath. 'So, are you going to tell me her name or not?'

He felt a weird stirring in his chest. 'It's Tommie.'

'Unusual…'

'Named for a great-aunt, apparently—Thomasina.'

'I prefer Tommie.'

'She does, too.'

'Right…' Felicity was sliding into distracted mode. 'I've got stuff piling up here, so I'd better shoot. I guess I'll see you next month at the wedding?'

His ribs tightened. Cousin Lucy's wedding to Fraser Pringle. Two hundred guests. Including his parents. He pushed the thought away.

'Yep. I'll see you there.'

'Great! Take it easy, Max.'

And then she was gone.

He put a finger to his cup handle, pushing it back and forth, watching the cup twist. How were things going in the annexe? Was Tommie all moved in now? Was she comfortable? Happy?

Gah!

He got to his feet and went out onto the deck, drawing the sweet grass and honeysuckle smells into his lungs. Of course she was happy. She'd stung him for more money and was now moving into a luxury apartment equipped with all the mod cons. No earthly reason for her not to be. And no earthly reason for him to be thinking about her—not when he had more important things to think about, ducks to line up in a row for tomorrow. Wall-to-wall meetings—back to business!

He felt his focus sliding down his left arm. Back to business with this lame appendage. Attracting attention, pity, questions he couldn't answer.

He shuddered. *Nightmare!*

CHAPTER FOUR

TOMMIE GLANCED INTO the rearview mirror. Was this a dream she was having? Monday morning. Six-thirty. Maxwell Lawler Scott back there, clean-shaven, with his hair brushed and swept back off his forehead, wearing a dark jacket over a white vee-neck tee and dark *proper* trousers—which must have been a devil to get on one-handed—looking extremely handsome, every inch the hotshot billionaire, while she, Tommie, was behind the wheel, driving him to his Canary Wharf offices!

She gripped the wheel harder. No, not a dream—and so *not* the way she'd thought this would play out. Billie's fault! Okay, maybe a little bit hers too, for falling head over heels in love with the annexe.

Oh, she'd known it would be gorgeous, but she hadn't expected it to take her actual breath away, shred every last vestige of her composure. Space, light, air… The apartment was a sublime echo of the main house. And such a bedroom!

All natural tones and deep-sprung comfort. Such a bathroom! All buff tiles and gleaming white porcelain.

How was it possible to keep your guard up when everything you were seeing was pure delight? When your delight seemed to be pleasing the other person? Not that pleasing Max had been her aim, and not that he'd exactly shown that he was pleased, but there'd been something intriguing going on behind his eyes. A sort of look behind the look.

He'd shown her more than the annexe, anyway, which she hadn't expected, making a few gruff remarks about the house's design and ecologically sound materials as he went. Gym. Lap pool… *Spa vibe central!* He'd said whoever got the job would be able to knock themselves out in there, since he was out of action. Then it was the garage. No rusty barbecue on wheels. No rolls of old carpet. Just three sleek sports cars and this one—this black, top-of-the-range hybrid four-by-four that smelt of its butter-soft leather interior and drove like a dream.

She just hadn't imagined that *she* would be the one driving it. Because Max had asked the agency to send three further candidates for interview after her—not that Billie was meant to have known it was Max who was asking. But stuff the non-disclosure agreement! After the interview she'd had to call her sister to let off steam, tell her that the prospective employer was Chloe Mills' damn publicist, and that she'd nearly died when he'd opened the door...

'Oh, my God—but Max Scott is gorgeous! Sex on a stick. Was he nice?'

'Not exactly. He was stiff, standoffish, and even though his hand's in a splint, because he bust it in a car crash—which is why he needs a driver— he insisted on getting me a glass of water, even though I offered to get it myself, which would have been a lot easier.'

'But that's kind of adorable...'

'No, Billie! He wasn't being adorable. It was a pride thing. He didn't want me to help him. He wanted to show off instead. It was so ridiculous, so stupid! Why not accept help?'

'Well, maybe because being helped makes him feel worse. Not independent.'

'Okay...maybe... But, see, that's still down to pride. I helped in the end—forced the issue.'

'Attagirl. How did it go, otherwise?'

'I endured, answered his questions, did my best not to show the agency up.'

'And what about the set-up? The apartment? Decent?'

'As expected, it's to die for.'

'*So, if he offers you the job, you're taking it, right?*'

'*I can't. This is Chloe Mills' publicist, remember?*'

'*So you'd cut off your nose to spite your face? Not take a brilliant job with a drop-dead gorgeous man just because Chloe Mills happens to be one of his clients?*'

'*Drop-dead gorgeous is irrelevant, Billie! This is a job, not a dating show, you know. With professional boundaries and everything. If I was working for him, he might just as well be Quasimodo.*'

'*Okay, well, obviously there's that. But since he isn't, at least you'd have a nice view in the rearview mirror!*'

'*I'm not interested in the view.*'

'*Funny…that's not the vibe I'm getting.*'

Billie had been barking up the wrong stupid tree. For sure, she'd felt a bit sorry for Max, with his hand cased up like that, and he had looked quite appealing, trying not to chuckle over 'Thomasina', and, yes, seeing that had made her a bit curious about him and, for heaven's sake, a girl would have to be dead on a slab not to find him attractive, but it didn't mean she was interested in Max in that way. He was from a different world socially. He was prideful, uptight *and* Chloe Mills' publicist. He was also beside the point, since she was fully focused on higher goals—in other words, herself.

It was the house, in particular the apartment, that had broken her. It had felt like home straight away—a place she could see herself in, sketching, researching, swanning around doing her own thing. *That* must have been the vibe Billie had picked up—apartment infatuation!

Neither here nor there, though. She'd written the whole thing off when Billie had told her Max was interviewing other people. But then, out of the blue, Billie had called her at work...

'Guess what? Max called Neville. You got the job! He wants you to be his driver!'

'No...'

'Yes!'

'How come?'

'Well, I'm assuming it's because he'd didn't like the other three as much as he likes you... Tommie? Are you still there...? Say something? What should Neville tell him?'

'I don't know.'

'Oh, for God's sake! You're not still stuck on the Chloe Mills thing, are you?'

'I don't know. She stole my designs, Billie, and he's on her team. And he doesn't even know I worked for her—'

'He doesn't have to! Geez, Tommie. Are you going to let Chloe Mills shaft you twice? Stop

*you taking a job that could set you up, give you
another crack at the dream? You don't have to
tell him anything...you don't even have to talk to
him. All you have to do is drive his car.'*

'I know, but—'

*'Would more money sway you? Make the pain
worth the gain?'*

'No, it's not that. It's just—'

*'Leave it with me. I'll tell Neville you're haver-
ing because you had a slightly higher figure in
mind. He loves to negotiate up because it's more
commission for him. If Max bites, then there's
your compensation for suffering the Chloe Mills
connection. If he doesn't, then we regroup...'*

But Max did bite. And she'd listened to Billie, got her priorities straightened back out. Max
was an unfortunate fly in the ointment, but so
what? The ointment was the thing. The job was
still the same job she'd gone off that morning
desperately hoping to get—for the money and
for the blissful bonus of having her own little
apartment.

She flicked the indicator, merging the vehicle
into the flow of slowing traffic. So here she was,
and there he was in the back, staring fixedly out
of the window, with a face on him like a wet
weekend. So much for Billie teasing her about
how readily he had shelled out the extra money

to secure her, saying how it must mean he liked her. If he did, he had a funny way of showing it.

He hadn't even come by to say hello when she'd arrived yesterday. Oh, he'd provided the lovely Isak to carry her stuff in, and the fridge had been full to the brim, stocked with expensive delicacies she wouldn't have bought for herself in a million years. And the bed had been made up, all ready for her. And the whole place had been spotless, which it had been the first time she'd seen it as well, but he'd clearly had it spruced up for her arrival. It had been a welcome of sorts—not lost on her—but he'd only shown his actual face later, seeming pleased to see her for all of three seconds before reverting to poker-up-the-jacksie mode, briefing her stiffly about today's trip to the Lawler-Scott PR and Alpha News headquarters—*'The other things I do besides wiping out in racing cars'*—and about how he didn't want or expect her to open the car door for him, or anything like that, that she was a driver *not* a chauffeur. Then he'd moved on to the cleaning and laundry arrangements—taken care of by someone called Jenny—and finally he'd given her a list of the local restaurants he had accounts with, so that she could order whatever she wanted, whenever she wanted, because *'You won't always have time to shop and cook.'*

It was all very thoughtful and efficient, but

he hadn't smiled once. And this morning he'd only smiled briefly as he got in and said hello. Since then he'd barely looked at her, hadn't said a single word to her. And she could hear Billie's voice in her head, saying that as a fully paid-up privacy nut he was probably just acclimatising to having her around, and her own voice adding that it didn't matter, she should just ignore him, but for some reason she was struggling to do that.

She checked her mirrors, slid over a lane. Was it because of that Thomasina moment and all those other little glimmers? That flicker of acknowledgement—*gratitude?*—in his gaze when she'd retrieved her water from the fridge door? That hard ache behind his eyes when he'd talked about his hand? That obvious warm affection for his sister, and that indefinable but arresting *something* at the edge of his gaze as he'd been showing her around?

Had her sappy subconscious decided they were signs of a potentially likeable inner being and woven them into some sort of loose expectation that they might get on? Even though getting on with Max wasn't important?

Who knew? She just didn't want to feel it buzzing away in her brain like this, taking up space when she had more important things to think about—like getting some ideas down for a Tommie Seager summer collection. She didn't want to keep looking at him in the mirror either, but she kept doing it all the same. Moth to flame, on account of his not being Quasimodo!

He was clenching his jaw now…rhythmically. Was he irked because he wasn't the one driving. Was she grinding his gears just by being here? *In. His. Space.* Nothing she could do about that, since she couldn't make herself invisible!

She looked again. Or maybe the jaw clenching had nothing to do with her at all. It could be work related…

Her breath checked.

Going back to work-related…

She glanced at him again. Was that what it was? First day back nerves? If so, she could relate. She'd hated going back to school after her glandular fever, dreaded the looks, the attention, the questions.

'Where have you been?'

'What happened to you?'

At least when she went back she was better, though…over it. But Max wasn't, was he? It was all still hanging in the balance for him. Her heart pinched. Much harder to deal with on a personal level, never mind in front of work colleagues.

She slowed to let a car filter in from the left. Oh, and now there was that voice starting up in her head, saying that it might help him to know she understood. What was it with her and wanting to help people all the time? It never ended well! She needed to steer well clear.

She concentrated on the road ahead. The traffic was building now—probably the Limehouse contraflow effect—but the road was pretty, with trees either side, blue sky above and soft morning sunshine. She felt a tingle. The weather! Now, there was a safe subject. Everyone talked about the weather, didn't they? It would be a little something to break the ice with…lighten the air. Max might even appreciate the distraction.

She drew in a breath and smiled into the mirror. 'You've got a lovely day for your first day back.'

His body tensed, then his eyes snapped to hers. 'Seems so. But I don't want to talk about the weather, Tommie. In fact, I don't want to talk at all. So if you could please not talk too, then I'd appreciate it.'

Seriously? Talking to her like this? Looking at her like this? Looking *away* now, back through the window, as if that was it—Tommie dismissed!

She felt a blaze reaching up under her ribs, then tears prickling, scalding her eyes. So much for good intentions. So much for trying to lighten the air. If Max was happier stewing in his own juices, grinding his own jaw to dust, then let him. At least she knew the score now. So, happy days!

She lifted her chin, breathing it all down. Made it easier, didn't it? Not talking. Not trying. Oh, and suddenly how very gratifying that Neville had put the squeeze on him for that extra fifteen percent! She'd never wanted it—had been too discombobulated about the job offer to make that plain to Billie—but she was cock-a-hoop about it now!

Money! That was the thing. Making enough to set herself up. Nothing else mattered—especially not Max Lawler Scott. She didn't need to talk to him…didn't need to be his buddy. All she had to do was drive his fricking car!

CHAPTER FIVE

MAX BLINKED. Where the hell was Tommie going? These buildings weren't familiar…and this road… This wasn't the right route!

His heart dipped. *Oh, God!* Now he was going to have to say something—look at her…brave the fall-out. And fall-out there would be, for sure, because her gaze in the mirror when he'd asked her to be quiet had solidified like cold metal. It would have turned him into a pillar of salt if he hadn't been feeling like one already, *this close* to crumbling along his edges.

Dammit! He'd intended to be curt with her, yes—to stop her in her tracks because he did *not* want to talk, engage. But he hadn't meant to be quite so obnoxious. It had just come out that way because he was in seriously bad shape: dreading walking into work, having to deal with the looks, the well-intentioned sympathy, the ignominy of not being fully himself, not being in total control. All that, while trying to fathom these very weird feelings he was getting around Tommie.

Not that he'd been around her much, but it didn't seem to take much.

Take last night… He'd gone up to brief her about today, full of clean slate intentions, and she'd opened the door balancing an armful of magazines on her hip, wearing low-slung jeans and a tight white tee that skimmed her navel and left nothing to the imagination as far as the size and shape of her breasts went—small and pert— her hair swept up but coming out of its clip so that loose tendrils were grazing the side of her neck. She'd looked adorably unkempt, momentarily soft, all softly lit up, and he'd felt something stirring inside him that was like desire but different—a sort of unholy clamour in his chest. He'd wanted to take her face in his hands and kiss her…kiss her long and slow…stretching it out, sinking into it, diving deep, drowning…

Drowning! That was how it had felt, suddenly—as if he couldn't get any air into his lungs. As if he was losing control of his breathing, too—and *that* didn't even happen on the racetrack at one hundred and twelve miles per hour! He'd panicked, fenced himself off, cracked on through it.

Forget time-wasting pleasantries.

Forget smiling.

But he couldn't forget the feeling. The skew and twist of it. It had kept him awake all night, tossing and turning. Then, to crown it all, this morning he'd taken so long struggling to get these ruddy trousers on that he hadn't had time for a coffee—and he *hated* that. He needed his caffeine fix first thing otherwise it was bear, sore head...the whole nine yards. All of it together had got him out of whack, out of sorts and biting Tommie's head right off instead of just baring his teeth to protect himself, as he'd meant to.

And now, having said he didn't want to talk, having told her he didn't want her to talk either, he was going to have to engage—because God only knew where she thought she was going!

He looked at her. 'Tommie, it's *Canary Wharf* we're headed to.'

Her shoulders stiffened perceptibly, then released. 'I know that, Max, but there's road-works through Limehouse. You said last night you wanted to be in for seven-thirty this morning, so I assumed you'd rather I take you round them and get you in on time than get stuck in a contraflow. But if I've called it wrong, then I apologise.'

Tart tone. Strong whiff of *Sorry, not sorry.* But that was fine. If she hated him now, so much the better. It would keep her at bay...keep her eyes out of the mirror and out of his.

'No, it's fine.' He slid his gaze back through

the window, hating himself for playing the role he'd cast himself in. 'You've called it right.'

Called it right because she was a professional driver. She'd have checked the road reports last night, planned this route and probably a back-up too. She was a safe pair of hands. A pair of hands he could—*should*—trust. But she was dangerous all the same...wearing her loveliness as if she didn't even know it was there, making his blood quick-march. Asking her disarming, candid questions—making it run cold.

'Do you live alone?'

'What did you do to your hand?'

'What's the prognosis?'

She'd been gearing up for another round, hadn't she? Stapling that *'first day back'* remark to a banal nicety about the weather. But he was on to her.

He shut his eyes. The kicker was that for a nanosecond he'd felt a tug...a faint desire to confide in her, tell her how much he was dreading facing his colleagues today. But she'd have pressed him then. Would have wanted to know why it was such a big deal. And he couldn't have got into that—the whole ugly labyrinth. Couldn't have told her how he couldn't bear showing weakness because he'd spent too much of his early life feeling weak, diminished, discounted. How he couldn't let anyone in because letting them in meant letting go, trusting, putting your happiness and self-esteem into someone else's hands... Someone who might be always too busy to come and watch you at the go-kart track, too self-absorbed to flick you a crumb of genuine attention. Someone who might promise to take you, watch you, praise you, love you, then re-nege because every other damn thing was more important. Themselves. News Global.

All their cronies. All those parties. Shrill and braying voices reverberating through the house every weekend, all weekend long, when he was growing up, taking up every bit of room, every bit of air. Journos and politicians, advisers and schemers, insiders with the latest on whichever juicy scandal was kicking off at Westminster that week. Catnip to Fliss. Purgatory to him.

It had got so that he couldn't wait to fly the nest, free himself from the noise and everything that went with it. From the pain of always being last on his parents, Tamsin and Gerald's list, pain that had curdled into resentment.

Most of it had anyway. There was still some of the pliant material there, lurking in his shadows, but he didn't give it houseroom—that sting of their disappointment in him for not joining the News Global dynasty after journalism school, as Fliss had, for going into showbiz journalism instead of becoming a 'serious' journalist, for boosting himself from there into the 'trite' world of celebrity PR.

But if Tamsin and Gerald chose to be disappointed in him for starting what was now the top celebrity PR firm in London and for launching Alpha News, for becoming independently wealthy and influential in his own right—and a respected motor racing driver to boot—then that was their problem.

Their problem, not mine!

Now, a fortune spent on therapy later, he could say those words out loud, and mean them.

He opened his eyes, surveying the unfamiliar road. Houses. A church. Shops. But therapy could only do so much. It couldn't un-weld him from this habit of self-reliance, of wanting to be in control of his space, his emotions, the terms of his relationships—everything. It couldn't make him want to let anyone in…couldn't make him not be scared of doing that.

That was what he would tell Tommie if he could—that his bark was worse than his bite, that he barked out of fear, not loathing. But Tommie was his driver. An employee. Not a friend and confidante. He liked her more than he wanted to, and he did want to kiss her, long and slow, but she was a tangle he could not afford to get himself into, even in the privacy of his own head. A head that was busy thumping right now, craving caffeine and—

Hallelujah, there's a coffee place!

He leant forward. 'Tommie, pull over, please.'

'Where?'

'As close as you can get to Roasted Joe's.'

So, Max was craving coffee, was he?

She checked the mirror, not letting her eyes stray off-piste, then flicked the indicator. Hopefully it would put him in a better mood before he made his grand entrance at work—hoping this for his colleagues' sake, obviously, not his. He could drown himself in his cup for all she cared!

She braked smoothly, pulling into the lucky space that a delivery van had just vacated right outside, then killed the engine, keeping her gaze forward.

There was a sharp click—Max's seatbelt— then silence, hanging like a dead weight.

Then… 'Would you like something?'

She felt a hot ripple beneath her skin, instant pathetic tears burning behind her lids. How could a voice do that? Just by not being cold… just by containing the merest, tiniest sliver of something that at a distant push might be said to feel like an apology.

She swallowed hard, drawing a silent stream of air in through her nose, taking it into her lungs, willing it to even her out. She wanted to say no…wanted to say it with spite in her voice, to sting him like he'd stung her. But that would only feel good for a barbed instant, and it wouldn't achieve anything except possibly to lose her this job. And she couldn't risk that— losing the money and the gorgeous apartment that already felt like home.

She drew in another long stream of air. No. The best payback was to stay professional, keep on taking his money, and do as little as possible for it—which, of course, ruled out offering to go and get the coffee. She felt another tingle. Or rather, *coffees*—because, actually, although she didn't like driving with a hot drink in the cup holder, she might make an exception this once for the sheer unadulterated pleasure of watching him work out how he was going to carry the damn things.

It was so perfect she could weep for joy. But only inside her head. Obviously.

Poker face, Tommie…

She inclined her head towards him without looking at him. 'That would be great, thanks. Tall Americano, please. Hot milk, no sugar.'

Nice and unwieldy!

'Got it.'

And then the door sprang open, letting in a whoosh of road noise before shutting with a soft *clunk.* She held her breath, counting to ten, then allowed herself to look.

Max was standing at the counter, giving his order to a female barista who was clearly smitten, batting her lashes at him, smiling and laughing—*gushing*—and falling over herself like a total twit. And Max was—*stop press!*—smiling back at the girl, with actual dents in his cheeks and everything. He was gripping the back of his neck now—which he had to know was a very disarming gesture, making him seem a bit shy, a smidge vulnerable...

She tore her eyes away. Oh, here she was again—tuning in to all the wrong things about him, imagining shyness, vulnerability, looking through the damn window in spite of herself, not to crow, not to gloat but—*admit it*—to see if he did actually need her help.

She sucked in her cheek, biting it hard. If only she could make herself not want to help people—but it was instinctive. It was who she was. She could rant and rail inside her head all day long, try on spite for size, but even though Max had been rude, and obnoxious, the fact was he'd been through a lot.

She felt a shudder rolling over her. She'd watched his crash online last night—watched his car flipping, rolling, five, six, seven times before ploughing to a dismembered, upside-down stop on the grass. And then the marshals and the medics had come swarming in, with the commentator describing the scene in a breathless, overawed voice, saying that the car would have taken the bulk of the impact, but for all that sounding keyed-up and anxious. And then the crowd had parted and there was Max, on his feet—white helmet, blue race suit—walking away, clutching his left hand. The commentator had been euphoric then. Max was okay. Walking away meant that he was okay.

But he wasn't. She'd seen the devastation behind his gaze when she'd asked him about the prognosis that day, had caught fear in his voice as well as bitterness.

'I can't feel anything...don't know when or if I ever will again.'

That was why she'd looked through the café window—because, no matter what had gone down between them earlier, he could only use one hand right now. And, yes, he'd probably rather die than ask her for help, but what kind of cold-hearted person would she be if she were to let him struggle?

She turned to look again, and felt her stomach spasm. He wasn't struggling, though, was he? The gushy barista was pulling the door open for him, all pink-cheeked and flirty smiling, hand-ing him a cardboard tray with two white-lidded cups secured in its slots.

Of course.

It was the obvious solution—one a smart billionaire hotshot like Max would have seized on before he'd even got through the door. Because you didn't get to be a business success, a billionaire in your own right, independently of your estranged billionaire media mogul father—she'd looked that up too, and some other things—by not being able to solve problems, grift when you had to, make nice with a barista to get attentive service.

From the hopeful look on her face, the silly girl was clearly hoping to get his number.

Not happening!

Max would no more look at that girl than he'd look at *her*. It was all on the internet, in the public domain. He had a 'type', pedigree racehorses one and all. Models, mostly, or actresses. Usually highborn. No one ordinary.

And now he was saying his goodbyes, turning, coming back across the pavement, tray in hand.

She composed her face, unclipped her seatbelt and got out, going round to open his door. Last night he'd said not to do that, but with the best will in the world he would never manage the car door without putting the tray down on the pavement first, and no professional driver would ever make a client do such a thing, no matter how trying that client was. And she *was* a professional…did have standards. But she wasn't going to smile. This was a bare minimum gesture, nothing more. Because whatever was going on inside her, whatever thoughts she couldn't seem to keep out of her head, Max *had* been brusque earlier, and unnecessarily rude. For self-preservation, and to stop all those other thoughts sending her down the usual road to disappointment, *that* was the thought she needed to hold on to with all her might!

CHAPTER SIX

'HOW'S IT GOING, MAX?'

He felt a little sinking sensation inside. Fliss wasn't asking him about work. She was using that sisterly tone of hers to go for his soft underbelly, using her *knowing* tone. But then, of course, she *did* know him—better than anyone. She knew he would have been struggling with himself this morning, with his various tics and demons, but surely she should also know by now that he was adept at hiding them, at controlling his own narrative.

Still, if she needed an actual run-down…

He leant back in his chair. 'It's all good, Fliss. I gathered the team together, told them that rolling my car hadn't been the most enjoyable experience but that my hand's still on the end of my arm, so it's not all bad, and that the rest is a waiting game. And then, of course, the Danny Gates thing kicked off, so it was action stations.'

'Fortuitous! Although not so much for Gates, obviously.'

'You saw it?'

She scoffed. 'Hard not to. Danny Gates and an escort! The socials are awash with it.'

He closed his eyes, trying to unsee the images. Danny Gates, until now a dream client, the nation's most popular kids' TV presenter, caught with his trousers down and a large-breasted woman in his hands. At various angles...none of them flattering.

'You did a nice quick mop up job on it, though, Max. Excellent admission and apology statement, and very smart to remind the nation that he's single, so there's no infidelity rap, and only twenty-two, so he should be forgiven for being an idiot. And that in spite of being *only* twenty-two, he's raised millions for children's charities.'

'Thanks, but it's standard procedure: admission, apology, then pile on the positivity. It won't save him his job.'

'No, but it'll save his career—which is what you're aiming for, right?'

'That's the hope. It's about the long game now.'

'So, what's next for Gates? A stint on *I'm a Jungle Star*?'

He felt his lips twitching. 'Ideally. Swallowing a mouthful of wriggling grubs seems to be a modern-day act of redemption—especially if it's followed by some tearful remorse for past wrongdoings by the campfire. His star will be shining again in no time. Then it'll be *Baking Blitz* or *Ballroom Blitz*—one of the primetime blitzes, anyway. I've already talked to his agent.'

Fliss chuckled. 'Sounds like you're all over it.'

'I'm paid to be all over it.'

'Don't be disingenuous, Max, it doesn't suit you. You don't need the money. You do it because you love it. And I'm not even going to start on *why* you love it…'

'Ouch, Fliss! You wouldn't be taunting me about my control issues, by any chance, would you?'

She laughed, but then her voice was softening, edging into seriousness. 'If not me, then who, Max? Who else is ever going to call you out?'

Who else would he ever let close enough to call him out? That was what she meant.

He felt a knot tightening in his chest. She was badgering him yet again with the same old chestnut—his refusal to let anyone in, open himself up to love. As if love was the answer to everything. As if just because she could do it—*was* doing it—sharing her life with Gavin, having a family, he should be doing it too. But they weren't the same. She had a natural resilience, had sailed through their childhood unscathed, whereas he'd had to cultivate his…grow it in sour earth. Different legacy. Different attitude.

Couldn't she get that, leave it alone? Leave *him* alone to simply be who he was?

'I don't need calling out, Fliss. I know what I am.'

'Do you, though?'

His body flashed hot. What was that supposed to mean? Not that he had any intention of asking her.

'I don't want to talk about this, Fliss.'

'You never do.'

'So why aren't you getting the message, then?'

'Nice!'

Grit and hurt in her voice. He felt the knot in his chest break.

'I'm sorry, Fliss, I didn't—'

'Forget it. I've got another call coming in. Have a nice rest of the day, Max!'

And then she was gone.

He clenched his jaw hard.

Good going, Max!

Upsetting Tommie. Upsetting Fliss.

He slammed his phone down and got to his feet, pacing the room. But how was he supposed to react? Why was everyone always trying to help him? Swamp him with help he didn't want, hadn't asked for, didn't need? Couldn't they see he was fine as he was? What was this need Fliss had to 'fix' him? He'd done the therapy…got himself fixed as far as he needed to, wanted to.

As for Tommie... Flicking him glances from the second he'd got into the car, trying to— what? Break him down? All she'd achieved was to wind him up more, force him to keep his gaze averted. Oh, but she'd kept on looking over, hadn't she? He'd felt her eyes on his face over and over again. The tingle of her, the goddamn tug of her, messing up his messed-up head even more. But this was what no one got: even as he was stewing in that back seat, indulging in some private self-pity—what *should* have been private self-pity anyway!—he'd known exactly how he was going to present himself when he pushed through the doors of these offices... known exactly what he was going to say. Because that was his talent. Controlling the narrative for his clients, and especially for himself.

He stopped pacing and turned to the expanse of London that filled the vast plate glass window of his office. Couldn't seem to control it around Tommie, though, could he? Offering to get her a coffee, hoping she'd read amends into it—and this after deciding that if she hated him it was for the best. Then flirting—yes, *flirting*—with that barista, hoping against hope—*why?*—that Tommie would be looking, noticing, feeling jealous. Which was insane. *Insane!* His driver. His employee. So far off limits it wasn't true. Not any kind of situation he wanted to get himself into. Oh, but there he'd been... Out of control, unable to stop himself, employing every disarming trick he could think of, making a total goof of himself, making that poor girl blush and simper, think that—

He screwed his eyes shut, grinding his teeth. Out of character. Not him at all. Some other Max. An alien being. He drew in a deep breath, reconnecting with the view. Luckily Tommie had missed the whole excruciating performance—which he knew because he'd checked a few times, and every time she'd been in the same pose, staring ahead, obviously still ticked off with him for jumping down her throat in spite of his peace offering—tall Americano, hot milk, no sugar.

She'd been on the pavement, opening his door for him, when he got back with it, saving him some awkwardness, but she'd taken it with the scantest 'thanks', not even popping the spout on the cup, just wedging it into the cup holder untouched as she slipped behind the wheel again. If that was a message, he'd got it. And it was absolutely the perfect outcome. Short shrift suited him down to the ground. Nothing to snag himself on, or to tug at the strings that had kept him awake all night. He was good now...back in control...

Golden!

CHAPTER SEVEN

'So, Danny Gates, huh…?'

Tommie felt her forehead wrinkling. 'What?'

'Oh, come on…' Billie's voice was cajoling. 'I *know* you've signed an NDA, but I'm dying to know: did Max tell you anything? I'm not asking for specifics, I just want to know: *was* there more?'

She put Billie on speaker, so she could plump her pillow and snuggle back. 'I don't even know what you're talking about.'

'Really?'

'Yes! *Really.*'

'Cripes! You're telling me you didn't see the pictures? Danny Gates, caught *in flagrante* with an escort. The media's been buzzing. And Max is Gates' publicist. He put out a statement…' Billie made a little impatient noise. 'And this has all somehow gone right over your head?'

'Well, obviously…'

And not surprisingly, since she was steering well clear of her computer and the internet

search app on her phone. Too tempting to look
up Max facts—like the fact that his sister was
Felicity Hewitt, anchor for News Global. Too
tempting to trawl through pictures of him, handsome and smiling, at red carpet events, at the
racetrack, at Wimbledon… Not that she would
tell Billie her guilty secret. It was bad enough
living with it herself, trying to make sense of
it. As for Max filling her in on anything about
his work… It might as well be his tongue in a
splint, not his hand.

'So Max didn't mention it?'

'Why would he? I've told you before: he's the
strong, silent type.'

'You mean still…?' Billie sounded incredulous. 'But it's been a week now. Isn't he loosening up a bit? Are you guys not—?'

'No, we're not friends. And before you ask,
yes, I'm fine with that. He's easy on the eye,
but in every other respect he's difficult. And I
don't care for what he does…oiling the wheels
for the likes of Chloe Mills, covering up for
Danny Gates.'

'The statement wasn't trying to cover anything up, Miss Know-it-All. It was actually an
apology.'

'Yeah, right. I'll bet "error of judgement" was
part of the script. It's what they always say when
these people do bad stuff.'

'Geez, Tommie, when did you get to be so prissy? Gates had consensual sex with someone, that's all. He didn't ask to be filmed doing it. He's actually the victim here. Max was trying to limit the damage—which in my book makes him quite noble.'

'There's nothing "noble" about it, Billie! He doesn't do it for free! hang on—' Her phone was vibrating with an incoming call.

Max!

'Sit tight, Billie, he's calling…' She inhaled and switched calls. 'Hello Max.'

'Hi, Tommie. I need to go out. Can you be ready in ten minutes, please?'

Seriously? Just when she was all tucked up in bed. Then again, this was what he was paying her for, wasn't it? To be at his beck and call.

She dialled up her professional tone. 'Of course. Where are we going?'

'The Dorchester. I'll see you out front.'

'Okay.' She switched back to Billie. 'We seem to be going to the Dorchester. He wants me outside with the car in ten minutes.'

'Ooh!' Billie's tone turned to honey. 'What's our boy going off to do in a luxury hotel at this time of night?'

Tommie felt a lurch inside. 'Don't know, don't

care. But I've now got nine minutes, forty-five seconds to be in place.'

'Go, then! You can tell me all about it tomorrow.'

'NDA, Billie… NDA. Bye.'

Thirty seconds later she was getting dressed. Fresh white shirt. Tailored grisaille cropped trousers. Pointless, really, since it was dark and no one was going to see her. But she had standards. Hair—quick twist up into its chignon. Face—quick once-over in the bathroom, lipstick…

She met her own eyes in the mirror. Did Max have standards though? Was Billie, right? Was he really going out to…?

She felt a sudden throb between her temples, a sick stirring in her stomach. How could he do that? Let himself be that guy? And why was she letting it bother her?

She pulled in a breath.

Whatever, whatever, whatever!

It didn't matter what Max did, day or night. His body, his choice. And was it really such a surprise? He had a playboy reputation, after all, and there was usually no smoke without fire. And he wasn't in a relationship…didn't want anyone living in his house, cramping his style, didn't want to *share* himself with anyone. He was selfish like that. He was also a hot, successful, single, virile billionaire player. It totally stacked up that he would do this kind of thing!

She rammed her feet into her shoes and went to stuff her sketchbook into her bag. Might as well use the booty call waiting time to work on some designs, try and distract herself from…

Oh, God! Maybe it did stack up, but didn't Max know he was better than this? Couldn't he see that he was selling himself short? *Gah!*

And there she went again, crediting him with way more than he deserved because, whatever she'd said to Billie, she *wanted* to see the good…, believe it was there in him. Glimmers getting into her eyes again, that beat of silence in the car that had felt like regret. That *'Would you like something?'* that had felt like an apology. And if he had been trying to apologise, then that pointed to some sensitivity in him, some good stuff, so why not share that good stuff with someone? Have a real relationship…something warm and tender, deep and joyful? If only she could talk some sense into him…make him see—

Stop!

She snatched up her bag, heading for the stairs, taking them fast. What the hell was she *on*? She couldn't talk to him. This was Max!

Into the garage now, past the gleaming row of cars to the four-by-four. She zapped the remote and got in. She'd paved that road with all her good intentions before, hadn't she? Just to lighten the air in the car, lighten him, and she'd got her head on a plate for her trouble. So, time to take a breath, take inventory.

Yes, Max had bought her a coffee to apologise—*perhaps*—but he hadn't *actually* apologised. And, whatever smidgeon of regret he might have been feeling when he'd offered to get it, it couldn't have been weighing on him that heavily, since ten seconds later he'd been in full spate, flirting with that bloody barista! And maybe he *hadn't* been rude to her again this week, but he hadn't made any effort to engage either. He'd just issued his polite back seat instructions: 'Kensington Mews, please, Tommie.' Or, 'Staverley Gardens, please, Tommie—physio appointment.' As if she even needed to know that... And, yes, she'd felt her heart going out to him because he'd looked rather downcast when he came out, but still, he was being attended to by a top post-operative specialist physio—she'd hopped out to read the brass plate by the door while he was inside—so he was luckier than most. And, downcast or not, he'd had a whole week to ask her how she was finding the apartment, ask her about anything, but he hadn't.

She triggered the garage door, watching it rise, then eased the car out.

Good pep talk, Tommie!

So many reasons not to care a fig about Max. Let him get on with it. His body. His choice. His life. Nothing to do with her. All she had to do was belt up and drive!

Max slid in, pulled his door shut. 'I'm sorry it's so late.'

He wasn't waiving his quiet in the car policy, or anything, but he couldn't *not* apologise for dragging Tommie out at getting on for eleven-thirty at night—not after upsetting her on her first day like that. For sure that unfortunate little episode had kept them suspended in a polite manageable silence which suited him down to the ground, and kept all those weird drowning-type feelings at bay, and for sure he was paying her extremely well for doing exactly this kind of thing. But still, given that he wasn't exactly overjoyed about traipsing out to the Dorchester at this time of night himself, odds were she was feeling the same.

'It's fine.'

Her eyes flicked him hard in the mirror and then she was easing the car through the gates and they were off, turning out onto the road, picking up speed.

Saying 'It's fine' but her tone implied the opposite—and her demeanour.

He tapped his fingers on the seat. He didn't

want to encourage conversation, and maybe it didn't matter that she didn't know *why* he was heading off to the Dorchester since he didn't usually tell her why they were going anywhere. Although for some reason he *had* told her he was going to the physio…maybe because they'd spoken about his hand at the interview, so it had felt all right to mention it. *Whatever!* But it *was* late, and she *did* seem ruffled, so maybe he should bend a bit…offer up some sort of explanation, some context. Brief, of course.

He looked into the mirror. 'This sometimes happens… Something blows up that needs a quick response. The socials never sleep.'

Her body stilled momentarily and then her eyes came to his. 'So this is a PR situation kind of thing?'

'Yes…' And that was as far as he was going.

He turned his gaze through the window to show her he was done. The rest was his business…his problem to sort out.

A frantic Christy Blume, furious because rival supermodel Luna Sanchez had just put out on social media that, at an event they'd both attended earlier, she'd overheard Christy saying that Crème de Zeus, the luxury American skincare brand Christy was ambassador for, was 'no better than the cheaper brands', and that it was the same stuff in superior packaging!

A case of the usual drill. Off to the Dorchester—his go-to neutral but suitably luxurious buffer space—to meet Christy, her manager and
her legal bods, to pull a damage limitation PR
response together before morning alarm clocks
started going off Stateside and Christy found
herself dropped.

He rolled his head back against the rest, closed
his eyes. What a week!

Upsetting Tommie on her first morning…up-
setting Fliss the same afternoon. Then Danny
Gates had upset the whole damn applecart with
that escort. And then Paul, his new physio, had
upset *him* at their very first session by stressing *degrees* of recovery over *speed* of recovery.
Not that he'd been getting his hopes up about his
hand, or anything, but somehow hearing all that
slow, cautionary talk, the same stuff the surgeon
had said weeks ago, had knocked the wind out
of his sails, brought back the grim reality that
he might never fully recover, never race again.

And now there was this Christy Blume situation!

He sighed and looked out through the window.
At least Tommie wasn't coming back at him, trying to talk. She seemed to have cottoned on to
his signals, decided he wasn't worth her trouble.

Oh, God! If only she knew he was shamming,
playing a role—and not because he didn't want to

talk to her, but because he did. *That* was the problem. *That* was the cat scattering his pigeons. How was he supposed to control this? This feeling of wanting to know her—know her properly—and be known by her in return. It was new...disconcerting, inciting bizarre behaviour like flirting with baristas. And he didn't want to be feeling these things, period, never mind feeling them about Tommie. She was his driver, for goodness' sake, his employee.

Oh, but for some reason he couldn't stop his mind from replaying that moment at her door, the day she moved in—couldn't stop himself wanting to relive the rapture. Time slowing to a crawl, his eyes taking in all her little nesting touches: photo frames set out neatly on the shelves, a blue throw folded and draped over the arm of the sofa, piles of magazines neatly arranged on the coffee table, taking in *her*—the slow, breathless rise and fall of her body, magazines stacked on her hip, her warm, pleased gaze reaching right inside him, that sweet golden skew of her hair, that soft cling of her tee shirt. That sudden, rushing, desperate urge to take her face in his hands and slow kiss her mouth, pour himself into her to the last hopeless drop—

'Max...?'

Tommie! In a somehow stationary car! Twisting round to look at him, her face golden in the lights of the hotel entrance.

'Do you know how long you'll be?'

How were they here already? And was it his imagination, or was her gaze a little gentler than it had been of late?

He shook himself, shrugging the thought away. 'That's the million-dollar question, I'm afraid. Lots of voices in the room and all that. Could be a couple of hours. You can give the keys to the valet.'

Her eyebrows flicked up. 'The valet?'

'Of course...'

His heart paused. Or maybe it wasn't obvious to her at all. And he'd never even thought to mention it, had he? Because he wasn't used to having to explain this stuff to anyone—let alone to a female driver who obviously needed to be given extra consideration as far as night-time safety went.

Must do better, Max!

He refocused. 'I'm sorry if that wasn't clear. For future reference, whenever we go out late at night, if there's valet parking, we'll always use it. And if there isn't...'

What then?

He licked his lips quickly. 'If there isn't, I'll walk with you from wherever we park so you're not walking alone. And late at night, wherever

I am, you must always come inside to wait—
okay?'

'Okay.' Little smile. 'Thank you.'

'You don't have to thank me. It's…' He bit
down on his tongue. He'd been going to say *common courtesy*, but since he hadn't exactly been
a model of courtesy that first day, common or
otherwise, it wouldn't cut any ice.

Move on!

He signalled to the doorman to come and open
his door, then looked at her again. 'I have a tab
here, so whatever you want food-wise, drink-wise,
knock yourself out.'

'Thank you.'

God help him, her gaze was opening into his,
tugging him into the vortex again.

Time to bail…get himself out of this car and
up to Room 452!

Tommie turned her face into the pillow. What
was that soft clinking noise? Familiar… Metallic… And what was that aroma? She tried to
concentrate on it. It smelt…almost like…

Coffee!

Her eyelids sprang open. Cups. Saucers.
Cafetière. Set out on the low table. And Max,
at an odd angle, regarding her from the opposite sofa.

Sofa?

She glanced at her pillow.

Oh, God!

Not a pillow but a cushion—the cushion she'd pulled under her head as she'd felt her eyes drooping. This was still somehow the same night…still the Dorchester Hotel!

His eyebrows lifted. 'You're awake.'

She felt a fire blazing up under her ribs and scrambled upright, thrusting her half-open sketchbook back into her bag, raking at her hair with her hands.

Had he been watching her for long? Had he seen her sketchbook? What must she look like? What must he be thinking?

He gestured to the cups as if he wasn't thinking anything at all. 'Have some coffee.' And then he was leaning forward, pulling one of the cups over to his side of the table, lifting it to his lips. 'It'll set you up for the drive back.'

Gah! Which was only bringing back every excruciating second of the drive here, trying— *failing*—not to think about what he was heading out for, only to find she was wrong, only to then wonder if he was saying it was a PR thing to cover up the *actual* thing that he was doing which was the thing Billie had said—*hating* herself for wondering about it, for letting it churn her up inside when it absolutely didn't matter. When Max was *nothing* to her, could never be anything to her, when she was supposed to be focused on herself and all her higher goals.

Only to find then, after all that stupid, incomprehensible anguish, that Max had been telling the truth. Easy to see in the proper light of the hotel entrance that his face wasn't the face of a man anticipating a happy frolic between the sheets but that he was here for the reason he'd given: work! And then he'd made his little speech about valet parking, and keeping her safe, with a sort of wounded protective look in his eyes, and she'd heard Billie's voice ringing loud in her ears about Max being 'noble' and it had suddenly felt as if it might possibly be slightly true.

And now here he was, with coffee *nobly* poured for her, when he probably just wanted to get home and crash. Because he looked done in, didn't he? Shadowy under the eyes and along his jaw, where new growth was coming in. He was in just his dark vee neck sweater now, sleeves pushed up a bit, jacket slung over the back of the sofa, and maybe it was the low light in the room, but he looked softer, sort of hazy and careworn. Maddeningly appealing.

Her heart lurched. Which was the last thing she should be letting herself think when he was sitting right here in front of her and might see it on her face. The thing was surely to be *not* sitting here in front of him in this dim lounge, with these empty sofas all around, and the silence pressing in at whatever ungodly hour of the morning this was. The thing was surely to be moving, sitting safely behind the wheel with him safely in the back, and the sooner the better.

She dug out a smile. 'I appreciate the coffee, Max, but I'm wide awake now. I don't need it.' She put her hand on her bag to seem ready to rise. 'We can just go.'

'What? And risk you falling asleep at the wheel?' He made a little scoffing noise. 'No, thanks.'

'I *won't* fall asleep!' Couldn't he see that she was firing on all cylinders? Maybe if she plundered the well of her own crippling embarrassment… 'I had a nap.'

The corner of his mouth twitched. 'Even so, I think you should drink it…fuel up. It's pretty good coffee.'

As if to demonstrate, he took a sip. And then he was setting his cup down, pulling out his phone, parking it on his knee. His eyes glanced up. 'Excuse me a sec…' And then he was tapping at his screen, scrolling.

Was he playing power games to make her drink the coffee because he really thought she might fall asleep at the wheel? *As if!* Or was he genuinely checking something important on his phone?

Whatever! She tipped some milk into the other cup and sat back with it, sipping. Point to him: it *was* excellent. She felt a stir in her chest. And the view wasn't bad either. Max, hair awry from the hand he'd just pushed through it, deeply engrossed in whatever he was reading on his screen. Rubbing his thumb over his lower lip now…slow strokes.

She felt her eyes staring, a curl of heat unwinding inside her. It was wrong to be looking… watching. But how not to watch when she could feel every thumb-stroke, when the fantasy of it was giving her delicious up-and-down ripples inside. That mouth of his…those lips. So perfect. His nose was perfect too. Straight, not too thin, not too broad. As for those cheekbones, and those thick lashes, and those dark straight brows, and the way his hair was falling forward over his forehead…

Gorgeous!

Her heart pulsed.

But what was he on the inside? *Who* was he?

Another pulse.

And why was she even asking herself that? Just because at this particular moment he was choosing *not* to be his usual shade of sullen! *Geez!* Why did it take so little to throw her backwards? Get her looking for the good in him? Whatever he was—good, bad or indifferent—it didn't matter. The only thing that mattered was that he was her meal ticket. Her boss…

Her breath caught. Her very handsome boss. Who was somehow suddenly looking right at her, raising his very nice eyebrows.

'Okay?'

She felt warmth flooding into her cheeks, her throat turning to parchment. 'Mm-hmm.'

'How's the coffee?'

She sipped some quickly, so her voice would work. 'It's fine, thanks. Good.'

He nodded. 'Good.' He ran a tongue across his lip. 'The coffee's always good here. Special Colombian roast, or something.'

And then his hand was going to the back of his neck, giving him that open, vulnerable, appealing look he'd had with the gushy barista.

'There's more in the pot if you want.'

'No, I'm good…'

Seriously? How many times could two people say 'good' in the space of ten seconds? Stilted, much?

She felt a rise in her chest. And was it any wonder? From her side at least. Because what was his actual script here? Was he genuinely trying to be friendly, making an effort?

Earlier, in the car, telling her *why* they were

coming here, when aside from mentioning his physio appointment he'd never once supplied a reason for going anywhere before, apologising for the lateness, apologising for not explaining about the valet parking, then setting out what they would do in future when they had to go out late at night. Ordering this coffee for her, wanting her to drink it, and now he was sitting there—possibly against his own inclination, because he must be tired, possibly using his phone as a delaying tactic—while she did drink it.

To what end? Safety? Hers? His? Trying to show he was a good employer? It was quite the sea change, but why? What did it mean?

And now she was feeling like the proverbial cat on a hot tin roof, tongue-tied and wary in case—if she picked up the baton, made conversation back—she inadvertently pushed the Max button. Not that he looked wound tight right now…not like he had that first day…

Her stomach roiled.

Oh, to hell with it!

All this tiptoeing around not being herself was exhausting! He was a big boy. If he didn't want to talk, then let him say so. But she was going to jolly well pick up the baton. Because for one thing he was holding it out—albeit at half-mast—and for another, for good or ill, right or wrong, she wanted to know more about him, about who he was. If only to stop herself wondering about it…if only for a bit of peace.

She took a quick sip from her cup and smiled. 'So, how did it go with your PR situation? Did you save the day?'

His eyes filled with a momentary reluctance, but then he was releasing his neck, bringing his hand back down to his phone. 'I was just having a look.'

'And…?'

His lips set. 'The statement's getting some traction on the socials.'

Keeping going, Tommie…

'So, was it, like, a real emergency situation?'

He let out a short, wry laugh. 'What constitutes an emergency in PR terms wouldn't register on the scale of real emergencies—but if you count a damaging, unfounded rumour going viral, threatening a client's reputation and potentially a significant portion of her livelihood, then, yes, this was one.'

Such a grounded perspective on emergencies! Keeping his client's name private, but fully answering her question. She felt a warm swell of admiration, felt it rising into her eyes. He was good at this… Her heart squeezed. Oh, but he did look tired…probably wanted to get going. He was bending to his phone again now, which was maybe to make her feel that she didn't have to rush with her coffee, or maybe it was just that he wanted to look at his phone. Either way, it was beyond late.

She drained her cup and set it down. 'That's me done, so we can go. You can carry on with that in the car...'

His scrolling finger stilled, his whole frame stiffening. 'No, I can't.' And then he looked up, his gaze flat as glass. 'The phone slips off my knee.'

Her heart seized. *Idiot, Tommie!* How hadn't she put two and two together? Max never took out his phone in the car unless he was answering a call. *How* hadn't she noticed? All these things he was having to contend with—simple, everyday things she took for granted.

She looked at him, pressing her gaze into his so he'd know how terrible she felt. 'I'm sorry, Max, I didn't think. I was only thinking about how tired you look, that I should be taking you home...'

'It's fine—don't worry about it.' He looked down, closing his screen. 'We're both tired, so let's just get going.'

And then he was pocketing his phone, lifting his jacket, getting to his feet all in one swift moment, moving beyond the little two-sofas-and-a-coffee-table combo into the wider room.

Standing apart. Distancing himself.

She felt her heart sinking. Was this another sea change? A switch back? Or just tiredness at the end of a long day?

She reached for her bag and got up. Just when things had been feeling easier, more level... And, no, it shouldn't matter how level things were, because all she had to do was drive his car, keep taking his money and push forward with her plans, keep her eye on the prize. But for some reason, right at this moment, it did matter. Very much.

CHAPTER EIGHT

MAX DREW UP with a start. *What the...?*

Tommie! Sitting in Reception, legs crossed, sunglasses perched, absorbed in *Vogue* magazine as if this were a hotel lobby instead of a *private* physiotherapy practice. As if he wasn't a *private* patient attending a *private* appointment. As if he didn't want—*need*—a few *private* moments after his appointment to process and regroup...a few moments *not* to be burning at the end of her eternally questing gaze!

He reversed a few paces, leant back against the wall.

For pity's sake!

Was this his reward for trying to be the same with her as he was with his other employees? All he'd been trying to do with that coffee at the Dorchester last week was make amends for not briefing her properly about the night-time parking arrangements, for not even thinking about all the nuts and bolts of that stuff because of this constant ridiculous tailspin she had him in, this clamour that had him reverse parking into himself all the time, instead of dealing with practicalities.

That meeting with Christy Blume et al... Half his mind on the job, half on Tommie, on how he needed to get his act together around her, treat her like he did everyone else. Be a better boss, a better human. In other words, normal Max.

Coffee because she was out for the count...because he'd have done the same for any member of his staff, done it for Fliss. And, yes, watching her sleeping hadn't exactly been a hardship—because when did he ever get the chance to really look at her, enjoy the sweet sight of her? The neat arch of her eyebrows, the delicate line of her nose. And those lips...full, slightly parted in sleep. She'd looked loose-limbed, every contour soft, her hands, fingers, losing their grip on a half-open sketchbook. Pencil lines. Too dim in the room to see detail. Then she'd woken up, treated him to some quite amusing conniptions...

It had been fine. He'd had it all under control. For sure, he'd had to get out his phone, to show her he wasn't heading anywhere until she'd drunk the coffee, until she'd properly come back to herself and was fit to drive. And, yes, he had almost got too absorbed in checking the socials to see how the PR statement was tracking. But he'd pulled himself back to the moment, had a stab at conversation.

Catnip to Tommie, of course. Predictably, she'd started with her questions, her gaze opening out, and that had started the tailspin feeling. But he'd kept his cool, powered on through. And then she'd said that thing about how he could use his phone in the car, and it had felt like a lightning strike in his chest because that was another thing he couldn't do because of his hand. The worst thing, though, was the way she'd looked at him then, reaching right in with her gaze. As if she cared…could feel his pain and frustration. And he'd felt fear rushing into his head, grabbing hold of his mind, shouting, *No, no, no.* He didn't *want* anyone feeling sorry for him, especially her. He didn't want anyone seeing the fragile tips of him, seeing the pain, because that stuff was private, his alone. He was no one's sideshow.

He'd called time quickly, gone to chat to the night manager to level himself out while the car was being brought round. And maybe Tommie had read his mood, seen that he needed his own space, because she hadn't said much on the way home. And these past few days she'd been keeping to her corner…except for her eyes, that grey-green gaze. Always there whenever he looked up, trying to peel him open.

He ground his teeth. And now it wasn't only

her eyes but herself—here where she had no business being, here at exactly the wrong moment, when Paul had just rained—*no*, poured a fricking deluge—on his parade.

'Sorry, Max. The twinge in your palm is just that. It isn't a sign that the nerves higher up are repairing themselves. You've got to be patient, buddy. On the bright side, your bones are almost healed, so we can put you in a less cumbersome splint, air those fingertips...'

He looked at his hand. As if air made any difference! As if being able to see his fingertips made any difference. He couldn't feel them, make them move. He was still at base camp, and the last thing he needed—the very *last* thing he could cope with right now, when he was feeling this low, this frustrated, when he was patently *not* in control of this thing—was Tommie up in his face. God help him, he didn't *want* to upset her, but he couldn't make himself not feel furious. He couldn't have her waltzing in here like this—he just couldn't. She needed to know, to be told in no uncertain terms that she was not to come in here. Ever!

He drew in a breath and pushed away from the wall, striding back out into Reception. He sensed her gaze lifting, but he couldn't bring himself to look at her. He just kept walking, through the doors, through the lobby, and then he was at the main door, seizing the handle, yanking it open, stepping outside.

'Max?' She was a step behind, looking at him with wide, searching eyes. 'Are you okay?'

His heart kicked. Could those eyes really not see what was happening here? How she was pushing him to the brink, making him this person he didn't want to be? Chaotic. Emotional. Unable to hold back. Struggling to keep his voice level.

'No, I'm not okay, Tommie! Why did you come inside?'

She recoiled a little, frowning. 'To wait for you, of course...'

'You haven't happened to notice that it's a *private* clinic? Haven't processed that I was attending a *private* appointment!'

Her features drew in. 'But I wasn't *in* the appointment room, Max! I was *in* Reception.'

Seriously? Emphasising the word to him? Arguing semantics? Was she trying to make him crosser than he was already?

'I'm not asking you to state the obvious. I'm asking you *why* you were in Reception, where you had no business being, instead of in the car, where you should have been!'

Her eyes flashed. 'And asking rudely, it must be said!' And then her gaze flattened. 'Maybe you should look around you, Max, ask *yourself* the question. *Why wasn't Tommie waiting in the car?'* She jerked her head towards the street behind him, indicating where he should look. 'Go on—see if you can work it out.'

Glinting gaze…triumphant.

He felt his stomach tightening, dread circling. Why did it seem that he was about to be bested, humbled?

He swallowed hard and turned. Curved street. Railings. Communal garden. Two phone engineers bent over a junction box with a spaghetti of wires hanging out of it. Van alongside, doors open… *Oh, God.* In more or less the same place as—

Her voice wrenched him back, cutting the thought out from under him.

'Those guys asked me if I'd mind moving so they could get their van close to the box. And, believe it not, this being London, it wasn't that easy to find another parking space. I managed, of course, but it's streets away. I thought of texting you, to let you know, but then I thought about what you said the other night about your phone and your hand…'

The glint in her eyes faded for a second then relit, setting shame alight inside him.

'I thought that if you didn't know the street you'd struggle to use the maps app on your phone, so I came back to collect you. And maybe you'd have rather I sat down on the doorstep to wait, but I'm sorry, Max…' Her eyes were glistening now, driving in the knife, twisting it hard. 'Even for what you're paying me, I'm not sitting on any bloody doorstep!'

Words…ringing…reverberating. The sudden, awful dead weight of himself.

'I'd never ask you to sit—'

He bit down on his tongue hard. So *not* the thing to lead with! His heart pulsed. What the hell was wrong with him? And what was he doing, dithering about like this? From the look of her, she was *this* close to walking away—and he couldn't let that happen, couldn't lose her. Not this kind, thoughtful, professional, beautiful woman who'd come back for him when it was the last thing he deserved.

He pulled in a breath. 'I'm sorry, Tommie. I was out of order.'

Her mouth twisted. 'Not only that…'

Holding him at the pointed end of her gaze.

His heart pinched. 'And I was rude, yes…'

Her eyes confirmed that he'd hit the mark. Would his apology hit the mark too? Buy him forgiveness?

He shifted his stance. 'I'm sorry I was rude to you. I—'

Didn't have a leg to stand on was the honest truth, because the problem was all his, wasn't it?

Perpetually seeing The Inquisition in her eyes when it was—could only be—simple kindness, routine concern. Kicking off, pushing back against it, because accepting kindness and concern felt like an admission of weakness, an admission that he wasn't in control, that he was fragile and vulnerable, that he might actually need somebody.

He knew his triggers. Fliss had told him a million times what they were, and therapy had filled in the blanks. It was just that he wasn't used to *being* triggered. That was the difference with Tommie. The perplexing, agonising push and pull of her—sorting it out in his mind, separating the purely physical, sexual tug of her from the other, scarier one. That tingling, alien impulse to confide in her, trust her, dive into her ocean. A bad impulse. *Wrong!* Because she was his employee—his employee who was looking at him now, waiting for him to explain himself, maybe waiting to make a 'stay or go' decision on the basis of what came out of his mouth.

His heart swung. It had to be the truth. Not the whole private messy truth of himself, but everything else… He drew in a breath. 'I'm not trying to justify anything, because I can't. I was rude, out of order, and I'm sorry…really sorry, Tommie. I have some things to say though, if you'd please hear me out…'

She folded her arms, holding his gaze, and then suddenly something gave way in her eyes. 'Okay. We should probably walk and talk, though, since it's about twenty miles to the car.'

His heart lifted. Not words she'd be saying if she was about to quit on him. He felt a smile trying to come and held it in.

'Good idea.'

'Right.' She dropped her shades, adjusted her tote, and then she was off.

He fell in, matching his stride to hers. 'So... this isn't meant to be an excuse, but it's context, okay?'

'Okay.'

'The thing is my session back there didn't go so well.'

She glanced over. 'I'm sorry.'

'Don't be. It's my own fault. Remember at the interview how I said I didn't want to get my hopes up with this hand? That I needed to be realistic?'

'Yes! And I said you shouldn't let realistic become pessimistic.'

Verbatim!

'Well, seems I'm not much good at being either. I felt a twinge in my palm yesterday, and I went from nought to full-speed optimism in the space of a second. I thought Paul—he's my physio—would be full of happy news, but seem-

ingly a twinge is just that, doesn't mean a thing.
And then he gave me The Talk—you know...
"Be patient, these things take time." And then
it was the hopeful stuff. *"You're young, fit, your
chances are good."* Then came the usual warnings about *"no guarantees"*, and about how I
need to take one day at a time. Basically the
same stuff the surgeon said weeks ago. What it
amounts to is that I've made no progress at all
since the crash. And I'm not trying to make you
feel bad, but after I'd seen Paul I just needed a
bit of time...you know, to get over myself, pull
myself together.'

'Oh, God, and instead I was there!' She
stopped suddenly, pushing up her shades, filling his eyes with her gaze. 'I'm so sorry. I didn't
even think—'

'Would you please stop apologising? This
is me, trying to give you some context so you
understand, but it doesn't alter the fact that I
shouldn't have lost it, and I *shouldn't* have spoken to you like that. *None* of this is your fault,
Tommie. You didn't know. It's not like I briefed
you on the whole wait-in-the-car-because-this-
injury-is-testing-every-scrap-of-my-patience
thing.'

She blinked. 'Well, no, but I *did* wait in the
car last time, so you probably assumed I'd do
the same again.'

Cutting him some slack, being kind…

Her gaze cleared. 'Probably the thing to focus on is that I know *now* that you need some space after your session. So, if anything like this happens again here's what we'll do: I'll text you, right?'

He felt his head nodding. 'Okay.'

'Then, when you're finished, you can text me back, or call, and I'll come for you.' She scrunched up her face. 'I don't know why I didn't think of that this time, actually.' And then she was shrugging her shoulders, rolling her eyes at herself, looking completely adorable. 'Epic fail.'

Just 'epic' would do. His heart squeezed. Did she have the slightest notion of how lovely she was? It didn't seem like it—not like the women he dated. Their beauty seemed to float apart from the rest of them, exist as a separate layer of awareness. Whereas Tommie was complete…everything zipped into her skin. Loveliness, openness, kindness, thoughtfulness. No wonder he was in a whirl. His breath checked. A silent, staring, mesmerised whirl.

He shook himself. 'Hardly a fail. In any case, I think that gong already belongs to me.'

Her eyes smiled, registering his quip. 'Don't be too hard on yourself, Max.' And then she was dropping her shades, turning to walk. 'It must be tough for you. Very frustrating.'

'It is…' He felt a beat of hesitation. He didn't want to regale her with his woes, but if he'd forced himself to brave the swirl of her gaze from the get-go, laid a few things out about what he was dealing with, trying to cope with, it might have saved them both some grief. In any case, he was enjoying this…talking to her. Why not talk more? Hell, it might even do him some good to get this stuff off his chest.

He looked over at her. 'You never think, until it happens to you, how an injury can make it hard to do the simplest things. Every damn thing becomes an exercise, a problem to solve. Everything takes longer: showering, getting dressed. And some things you just can't do—like buttoning a shirt, lacing a shoe. As for opening a packet…don't get me started. And no disrespect, because I'm lucky to have such an excellent driver in you—' just so she would know he was grateful to her, sorry to his bones for being so obnoxious, and that he didn't take her for granted '—but I miss driving my own car. Miss racing. It would still be frustrating, even if I had an end date, but I don't. So there's that as well. No progress. No end in sight.'

'You've got a different splint on, though…'

Which sort of felt like a prompt.

He raised his arm to show her. 'That's because

my bones are nearly healed. Apparently, this is enough protection now.'

She took it in. 'It's less cumbersome, anyway, and if your bones are getting there I'd call that progress.'

'It doesn't make any difference if I can't *feel* anything.' He dropped his arm back to his side, allowing himself a bit of petulance. 'I'm still on the bottom rung, going nowhere.'

Her sunglasses glinted. 'Oh, look, see—there you go. You've got your pessimism back!'

'Very funny.'

She flashed a grin. 'You're welcome.' And then she was looking ahead again. 'At least you can see your fingertips now...*touch* them. You could try massaging them.'

'To what end?'

She shrugged. 'I don't know... It sort of feels like something that would help. Has Paul given you any instructions?'

'Not yet. If my bones are a hundred percent next session he's going to take me through some "active assisted" exercises.'

'Well, maybe when you start doing those you'll feel a difference.' She chewed her lip for a moment and then she pushed up her shades again, looking over. 'In the meantime, remember I'm right here if you need help with anything...' She broke into a smile. 'I'm a dab hand at opening packets and strong-arming lids off jars.'

His heart clenched. Lovely Tommie. Touching him to the core with her kindness. But he could feel resistance stiffening in his chest…could feel that fear reaching up into his mind again.

He looked ahead, fighting to keep his tone neutral. 'You're not my nurse, Tommie.'

Little pause.

'I wasn't offering to be your nurse.'

And now it was a main road, and the pedestrian crossing, traffic whooshing left and right, moments of glinting chrome and scrolling reflections.

Tommie pressed the button to cross and then she was turning, looking at him, her gaze soft and serious. 'I watched your crash online, Max, and I know it was horrific. Whatever you feel about it, and whatever you feel about your injury—anger, frustration, misery—it's okay to feel those things. But it's also okay to accept help sometimes. Whatever you think, it isn't a sign of weakness.'

'I never said it was.' For some reason, the only thing he could think of to say. And then something else crashed in, taking him by surprise. 'Thanks, Tommie.'

She broke into a sudden smile, her eyes filling with warm, lovely light. 'You're welcome.'

And then she was turning back to the road, adjusting her bag on her shoulder as if she hadn't just blinded him, taken his breath away.

'Right, only another ten miles to go.'

CHAPTER NINE

SUCH A LOVELY AFTERNOON! Blue sky. White clouds. Reflecting in the glass of the high-rise buildings all around. Faceted blocks of bright sky against a backdrop of even more sky. And somewhere inside the biggest block, behind one of those vast glass panes, was Max, busy doing his PR thing while she, Tommie, was busy not concentrating on the one-shoulder ruffled blouse she was supposed to be sketching!

She forced her eyes back to the page, drew a line with her pencil. *Gah!* Not right! The whole damn design was off. She flipped back a page. Same thing. *Wrong!* She flipped again. Also wrong!

Flip, flip, flip.

Wrong, wrong, wrong!

She flung the pencil down and reached for her cup. All wrong. Three hours sitting here on this café terrace and the only progress she'd made was through two tall soda and limes and a pot of tea!

She felt her eyes drifting upwards again to Max's glass tower. *Max!* He was the problem. Nothing new there. But he'd become a worse problem since last week's showdown, because sorting everything out afterwards had changed things. The lie of the land… Her heart squeezed. The way *her* land lay in relation to his…

She sipped her tea, cradling the cup in her hands. The problem was that it was impossible not to like the Max who'd emerged from the ashes after she'd well and truly put him in his place. And it was especially hard not to like— and not to keep remembering—the way his eyes had softened all the way into hers when he'd said, 'Thanks, Tommie' at that crossing. Genuine warmth there…gratitude, honesty, openness. It had felt as if all the glimmers she'd ever seen in him had come together in that moment and fused themselves into one brilliant light so she could see him—*really* see him.

She put her cup down. That was the moment she kept coming back to—the one that wouldn't leave her alone. She couldn't stop those fierce little claws in her mind scratching at it, wondering what it meant, what it could mean—that he could look at her like *that*, make her feel so…so drawn, torn, flipped and rolled. *Crashed!* And now—even though she wasn't looking for a relationship with anyone, when she was set on her own goals—she couldn't seem to stop her imagination from running off all the time into an alternative Max and Tommie universe.

No wonder there was no imagination left to put into her designs. No wonder she couldn't sketch anything right.

She picked up the pencil, flipped to a new page. It was annoying. *Distracting!* She didn't want to be wasting time and energy on pointless thoughts and stupid fantasies. Max Lawler Scott was not, and never would be, interested in her. Not in *that* way. She was a train driver's daughter from South London with an accent to match and not even two half-decent exam grades to rub together! She wasn't putting herself down, or anything, because she had big plans, big dreams. But facts were facts. Max was silver spoon, and she wasn't.

She drew a fresh line, then another, drawing a bodice.

In any case, Max wasn't the relationship type. He wasn't even interested in his thoroughbred women, was he? If he'd been the settling down type, wanted that kind of thing, he'd have been with someone by now…married, maybe. But he wasn't.

She drew another line.

It was sad in a way…a shame. Because even though he seemed to be quite messed up, and proud, not to mention touchy as hell, underneath it all he was a good guy…had good qualities.

She shortened her pencil strokes, drawing a frill.

For one thing he wasn't too proud to climb down, admit fault, apologise. And he had a lovely wry sense of humour that he didn't seem to mind turning on himself.

'I think that gong already belongs to me.'

She liked that kind of quip, the neat way he put things. It was right up her street, brought the smile out in her, because it was her sense of humour too.

She felt a smile coming. These past few days it was what they'd been falling into more and more. Quips and teases. Back and forth banter. It was fun. Irresistible! Her stomach swooped. But it was muddying the waters. And she'd tried reminding herself that Max represented the rich and shady, but she couldn't seem to make that mud stick any more, since what little he'd told her about what he did always seemed to involve helping people…saving them from themselves. And she'd tried reminding herself that Max was Chloe Mills' publicist. But all that did was stoke the guilt inside her because he didn't know she'd worked for Chloe, didn't know she was keeping it from him. It hadn't seemed important before, hadn't bothered her when he'd been shut off, staring out of the window, communicating in monosyllables, but now—

'Hey!'

What the…?

'Max!'

Here! How? *Why?*

Because he never did this—came down to the commercial levels where the cafés and shops were. He always texted to say he was leaving the office, so she'd be back at the car, ready to go, when he emerged from the lift. But now he was pulling out the opposite chair, sitting himself down, amusement playing through his gaze.

'You look shocked, Tommie.'

What did he expect, blindsiding her like this? Sketchbook open. Secret dreams on show.

She drew in a breath. Admission…deflection. The gospel according to Max. The publicist's way of handling awkward situations. Well, this here was the mother of all awkward situations, so…

'Of course I'm shocked. You coming down here is a very random act.' She smiled into his eyes, using the moment to close her sketchbook and draw it close. 'Not that it isn't delightful to see you.' Now the pencil. Casual little pick-up. 'So, what brings you to the Netherworld?'

The corner of his mouth ticked up and then he was glancing out at the dock, lifting his gaze to the sky, looking around. 'It's a nice day. I've been trapped inside, looking at it through the window.' His eyes came back. 'I just fancied a bit of fresh air, and you said earlier that you often come to this place, so I thought I'd have a walk, see if you were here.' He gave a little shrug. 'Come and find *you* for a change.'

God help her, those blue eyes, that face, that hair lifting a little in the rippling breeze. Too gorgeous, too distracting.

Time to cut loose.

She smiled. 'Well, you've found me now, so shall we go?' She put her hand on the sketch book, ready to slide it into her bag.

'Not so fast…' His eyes darted to it, then came back. 'I've seen you with that book before and I promise I won't be offended if you tell me to mind my own business, but I have to tell you, I'm curious…' A keen light stole into his gaze. 'Before you not so subtly closed it, I saw what looked like a terrific design sketch for a blouse?'

She felt her breath stilling. He *liked* her design? Thought it was 'terrific' even though it was all wrong?

So unexpected. So nice. Making her heart glow.

But she couldn't talk fashion with Max. Couldn't talk about her big, shiny dream. Because what if it somehow jogged his memory about that moment at Chloe's party? Brought everything crashing down? That critical omission, that little bit of dishonesty? Maybe her fessing up about New York was on the cards at some point, but she couldn't do it now—not when they'd only just found a rhythm, when things were good, pleasant between them. If he pushed her on this, all she could do was take what he'd seen and spin it into something tiny and insignificant…something that was happily also true.

She took a quick sip of tea and smiled. 'Thank you, but really, it's nothing.'

'It didn't look like nothing.' His hand gestured to the book. 'Can I see?'

Her stomach tightened. If she dug her heels in it would only make him all the more curious. Better to fold, downplay it, be casual about it.

'Sure…' She handed it over, opening it up for him.

He scanned the page. 'I like this…' And then he was flicking through, page after page. 'These are good, Tommie!'

Way to make her blush!

And then he was looking up, forehead wrinkling. 'What are they for?'

Honest face, Tommie.

She shrugged. 'They're for me. I make some of my own clothes.' And as luck would have it… She glanced down. 'Like this top I'm wearing.'

His gaze dipped for a long, tingling second, taking it in, then came back all warm. 'Very nice. I like that black contrast trim around the neck…the way it sets off the white…'

Her pulse pinged with joy. 'That's *exactly* the detail I changed from the mass market version they were selling in the boutiques!' The man had an eye—got it totally! She felt a smile breaking, the fire stirring inside her. 'That's why I design stuff. Why I sew. So much fashion fails for want of the right detail, or the right finish. And so much of it is shoddy. Clothes should fit well, flatter, last, but so much of what's out there doesn't tick any of those boxes. It seems like it's made for landfill, when that's the exact opposite of what we should be doing with our clothes. It drives me insane!'

He smiled. 'I'm getting that…'

Nodding, gazing into her eyes, then *at* her eyes it felt like, taking her in, all her bare surfaces, making heat curl and pulse low down in her belly like it did at the Dorchester that night when she was watching his thumb, his lips, his lovely, lovely mouth.

And then suddenly he blinked and looked down, closing the book carefully. 'Thanks for showing me this.' He offered it back across the table with a nod. 'I'm impressed.'

'Thanks, but like I said, it's nothing…'

Unlike the messy way he'd just made her feel. Could he see it in her eyes? On her face? His face was composed, every plane in place, as if the moment had never happened—as if he hadn't just set those claws off again, scratching in her mind.

His eyebrows flashed. 'We should go.' And then he was getting up, looking down into the glinting water of the dock. 'I've got to stop off in Belgravia on the way back, but it shouldn't be for long.'

'Okay.'

She slid the sketch book into her bag. Talking about Belgravia but not saying who he was seeing, or why. Completely normal Max behaviour! Looking about him now, looking controlled, calm, completely normal. Whereas she… She took a breath and got up. Had she imagined that moment somehow? Read more into that look than was really in it? Her stomach pulsed. She must have…

And now that she was on her feet he was turning, heading for the exit, attracting furtive looks from the women seated at the other tables. She set off, following, trying not to notice the lovely way his hair curled at his nape or the confident flow of his stride.

She must have. Must have. Must have!

And she had to stop her imagination doing

this—sliding over lines, causing mayhem. Because it was pointless, and not even anything she wanted—to get caught up, become embroiled in any kind of relationship. Especially one with her gorgeous, impossible boss. What she *wanted* was to put herself on the fashion map, make something of herself, feel the satisfaction inside that she'd achieved something in spite of the knockbacks, feel that she was truly as good as everyone else.

She straightened, quickening her pace, inhaling deep into her lungs. *That* was the thought those little claws needed to sink themselves into. Tommie Seager was going to make it, prevail, show the world just what she was made of!

CHAPTER TEN

'YOU SAID YOU needed some—'

Tommie's eyes quickly registered his naked upper half, then attached themselves, somewhat firmly, to the shirt he was dangling from his finger.

He felt a dip in his chest. She was uncomfortable, but what could he do? Last-minute decision. He couldn't wear his usual sweater-jacket combo to Lucy and Fraser's wedding, especially now that he was *sans* splint. Without that explanatory prop he'd likely come over as casual, disrespectful or lazy—and, given that this wedding was already set to be hell on a stick, why make it even worse for himself by committing a wardrobe *faux pas*?

And if Tommie was feeling uncomfortable, then it was worse for him, not being able to attend to himself, having to ask for help. Worse still that he was going to have to endure her at close quarters when she was looking even more gorgeous than usual today, in those neat black cropped trousers and that white sleeveless mock turtleneck top that showed off her smooth lovely arms. It was going to stretch his self-control in the downstairs department to the limits of endurance.

But what choice did he have but to push through? Try to make it as painless as possible for both of them?

'I'm sorry, Tommie.' He smiled to put her at her ease. 'I wouldn't be asking if—'

'Don't be sorry. It's fine…' She smiled quickly, then plucked the shirt off his finger, opening it out, lifting it high in front her face. 'I said I'd help you if you needed me to, and you can't do this yourself. Turn round.'

Sounding brisk, exactly like…

He felt a real smile rising and turned, poking his right arm into its sleeve, then the left. Then he turned back round again. 'You've got a bit of a nursey tone about you today.'

'Sorry about that.' Eyes down, she was pulling the two halves of his shirt together, doing a button in the middle. 'Just trying to get the job done.'

Focusing so hard on it that she hadn't got the reference. He wouldn't have minded, except that he was poking fun at himself here, trying to lighten her up.

'Tommie?'

Her eyes flicked up. 'Yes?'

'I was joking…' He raised his eyebrows. 'Remember how I said I didn't want a nurse?'

Recognition flickered in her gaze.

He tried a smile. 'I was trying to make this feel a little less awkward…'

'Ah…' She drew in a little breath. 'Sorry. I was preoccupied. I suppose I was thinking that since you never even came back to me on packets and jar lids, asking me to help with *this* must be a heavy deal for you, so you'd want me to crack on…get it over with.'

His heart squeezed. Thinking of him, of course. Maybe of herself a bit too. Because this wasn't 'packets and jar lids', was it? This was above and beyond.

Probably the best thing he could actually do was just let her get on with it.

'You're right. On both counts.' He lifted his chin, looking ahead. 'Feel free to crack on.'

Except that cracking on meant enduring this torture of movement. Air moving, churning up delicious little wafts of her perfume. Fingers moving, tugging the shirt fabric against his skin. It didn't take much to set his blood alight around Tommie. Christ, just watching her face, all that lovely animation when she'd been talking about fashion at Canary Wharf last week, had sucked him in, got him losing himself in her gaze, feeling heat pooling in places it had no business pooling, and all that with zero touching involved!

And now her hands were moving lower, pulling the shirt away from his body and towards hers.

Oh, God!

Was it because she could sense what her touch was doing to him down there? He clenched his jaw. He needed a distraction fast…a sexual buzz-killer. Oh! And what better subject could there be…?

He exhaled. 'I don't even know why I'm putting us both through this. It's not as if I *want* to go to this bloody wedding.'

Her fingers stilled. 'Why don't you want to go?' And then she was bringing her hands up to his chest, doing up a button, making the fabric tickle and tease, catch at his nipples. 'Don't you like your cousin?'

Focus, Max.

He shook his head. 'Yes…no, it's not that. Lucy's absolutely lovely. And, Fraser, her intended…he's decent. It's just that—'

What?

What was he doing? He couldn't tell Tommie about Tamsin and Gerald, about the way he didn't like being around them. Because then she'd ask him why, and he couldn't dig into all the whys with her. She was his driver, seemingly his dresser now too, *not* his therapist. His heart shifted. But that was the other tug of her, wasn't it? That incomprehensible *something* about her that made him *want* to talk to her, tell her stuff he'd never told anyone.

Such a relief, in the end, offloading to her about his hand, and it was a relief being able to talk about it every day, about every twinge, every little tingle, to get it off his chest, get her measured but always upbeat take on it.

But Tamsin and Gerald were a whole other can of worms. Talking about them, even to Tommie, would only rile him up, and riled up was not how he wanted to arrive at the wedding. Odds were he'd be leaving that way, so why start early? He bit his lip. But now he'd left 'It's just that' hanging, hadn't he? He needed to scoop it up, press it flat, leave nothing for Tommie to seize on.

He pushed out a sigh, going for a weary, slightly bored tone. 'It's just family stuff, you know—foibles and irritations.'

'Right…' She was at his top button now, hesitating, glancing up. 'Can you lift your chin so I can—?'

'Of course.'

He obliged, looking up at the ceiling, trying to block out the warm sensation of her fingers against his throat. But then suddenly they stilled.

'Didn't you say yesterday there were two hundred people going?'

'Yep.'

Her fingers carried on. 'Well, with that many people milling about, couldn't you, like, hide?'

Great minds!

'That's exactly my plan—find a quiet corner...' Unless Lucy had put him on a table with Tamsin, Gerald, Fliss and Gavin, in which case he was doomed.

'So you'll be fine, then...' Tommie stepped back, taking in his shirt front with her eyes. 'Right, you're done.'

If only...

'Not quite, I'm afraid.' He lifted his hands, flapping the cuffs. 'I need my cufflinks.'

'Oh, of course.' Her gaze flitted off. 'Where are they?'

'On the side table, there. With my tie.'

'Okay.' She made a pivot and went over, hanging the tie around her neck, bending to the box to free the cufflinks.

He followed, folding his left cuff as he went, to speed things up.

But then suddenly she was spinning round, head down, clearly unaware that he was there, and before he could move she was ploughing into him, breasts against his chest, hair in his face, in a soft, lovely explosion.

'Sorry. Oh, God, sorry!'

Pulling away, blushing, but it was *his* fault—
unequivocally!

'No, *I'm* sorry, Tommie. I was coming to
you…trying to be helpful.'

'But I should have been looking where I was
going!'

This whole crazy situation!

He looked at her, offered up a shrug. 'Maybe
it doesn't matter.'

Her eyes held his for a long, tantalising beat,
then softened with a smile. 'Maybe you're right.
Shall we just do the cufflinks?'

'Okay.' He held out his left hand. 'You'll note
I've folded the cuff, ready for you…'

She paused. 'Being helpful again?'

He felt a smile spreading into his cheeks. 'It's
the least I can do.'

She chuckled softly. 'Okay, well, the other
thing you can do is please hold still. Because
this is fiddly.'

And then she was pinching his cuff together,
sliding the cufflink in, giving it a twist.

'You're doing great…' He swapped hands.
'I'm very grateful, you know.'

Her eyes glanced up, twinkling. 'So you
should be.' Folding his cuff, fitting the second
cufflink. 'This is over and above, you know.'

His heart paused. Which called for something in return, didn't it? A thought to come back to.

'I'm aware, but thanks for the reminder.'

She stepped back, raising her eyes to his with a smile that had a touch of relief about it.

'Just the tie now. Windsor knot?'

'You read my mind.'

She grinned. 'Well, it's the best one, according to my grandad, so I figured that was the one you'd want.' But then she frowned. 'The only thing is, I can only do it on myself. So I'll do it three-quarters on me, then adjust it on you.'

'Whatever works. I'm in your capable hands.'

Hands that were lining up the tie now, expertly looping and threading. Hands that at any second would be around his neck from an up-close position, her body right there, her smell and her shimmering warmth putting him through the mill again.

And now she was stepping in, a flicker affecting her gaze. 'I need to stand your collar up...'

'Okay.' He straightened, lifting his chin, trying to hold his body away.

Last push, Max.

Hands, working his collar upright, fingers catching his hair at the back, shooting tingles through him. Moving round now, little brushes to his neck, jaw, briefly his cheek. He bore down. Could she hear his heart thundering? Feel the heat pulsing through him? Oh, and now she was lifting the tie over her own head, encircling him in her lovely smell, placing it over his head. Her face so close. Her lips slightly parted in concentration.

Torture!

Tugging, adjusting, her hands at his throat again. Top button…then reaching to the back of his neck again, pressing close, that little shower of her perfume, folding the collar down, working it round, eyes focused on the job, then moving back to the knot. One last adjustment and then she was melting back, a little breathless, a little blush in her cheeks.

'You're all done.'

Done for, more like—not that he could let it show.

'Thanks so much, Tommie.' He smiled, feeling the knot, which was spot on. 'You're a superstar.'

Her eyes lit with a tease. 'Too right, I am.' And then she was moving back a little. 'What time do you want to leave?

Now would be perfect, to steal a march on the weekend traffic, but he needed a moment to catch his breath—and from the look of her, Tommie did too.

He pushed his hair back. 'I've got a couple of

things to do before we go, so shall we say thirty minutes?'

'Great!' She seized the door handle, pulling the door open. 'I'll have the car outside for then.'

And then she was gone, leaving warm traces of her perfume behind her.

CHAPTER ELEVEN

TOMMIE FELT HER breath catching. 'Oh, my goodness, Max, this place...'

'Nice, isn't it.'

Nice?

She looked at him in the mirror. 'It isn't "nice"—it's blooming Pemberley; it's Mr Darcy and Elizabeth Bennet and Jane Austen!'

Three storeys of vast pale stone house, with a grand pillared entrance, immaculate lawns and terraces all around and wooded parkland beyond. Most likely there'd be a lake somewhere.

She slowed the car down so she could look properly, fill her whole gaze with it. Because if she did that, filled her senses to the brim, maybe it would push out Max and that whole shirt-buttoning business...

'Hey, Tommie, could you pop down a sec please...help me with something?'

No warning about what that 'something' was. He'd just opened the door and stepped back, parading his abs and his pecs and all those other muscles she didn't know the names of, dangling his shirt from his finger as if that explained everything. Which it had. And then it had been a case of girding herself, coping with that clean, fresh smell of him and that up-close heat radiating from him, coping with that crackling charge that had seemed to be there, skewing her senses and her hand-eye co-ordination, buttons slipping, fingers slipping. Oh, and then colliding with him like that! Coming up against that wall of chest and cotton and delicious heat. Cufflinks... Collar... Fingers trying, failing, not to catch his hair, his hot neck and his smooth, tense jaw. But it hadn't only been the sensory overload, it had been the looks, their little exchanges, that sense of...

And that sacred half-hour afterwards hadn't stopped her mind from swirling, and the drive here hadn't stopped it either. Because even though Max had been mostly quiet, preoccupied—undoubtedly with those so-called family *'foibles and irritations'*—which she knew from the internet were weightier than that—he was nevertheless right there on the back seat, looking impeccably, impossibly handsome, tugging at her senses like a great big bloody magnet.

Maybe getting out into all this space, walking in the grounds, communing with the trees in those woods, breathing in the bright green air, filling her senses with other distractions, would help her tamp these feelings down, stop her mind's eye seeing that tantalising, compelling light in his gaze and reading all the wrong things into it. Not only reading those things into it but, God help her, wanting them to be real, wanting *him*, wanting to know him, get close to him, *be* close to him, be someone to him, *something* to him…

She blinked, refocusing, turning the car onto the sweeping frontage, and then felt her eyes blinking again, a different focus arriving. Oh, what kind of fool was she, wanting 'real' with Max, feeding herself minuscule doses of a Max and Tommie reality, imagining that it could happen?

This was the reality check right here—all of this. This grand house, these lovely grounds, these sleek cars pulling up, these people getting out of them. Privileged people. Rich. Entitled. This was Max's world, wasn't it? He came from this. Not from this specific house, but from one like it—one that was nothing like the South London semi she'd grown up in, with neighbours, and barking dogs, and youths wheeling prams with the free papers in, shoving them through the door, half in, half out, making a draught whistle through the hall.

She braked, easing the car to a stop.

Different world.

'Right…' Max's belt unclicked and then he was leaning forward, so close, pointing through the windscreen, his cufflink catching the light. 'So, just follow those other cars to the western side of the house and park there. They want the front of the house left clear—for photos, presumably.'

Of course they did—a grand façade like that. She could imagine the photos already… Lucy in flowing silk and an heirloom veil, Fraser in tails and pin-striped trews, the pillars of the family pile rising in the background.

Different world.

Not hers. Not one she could ever belong to. That was the reality.

'Tommie…?'

She shook herself. 'Got it.'

'When you've parked, go round to the back. I believe they've made a sitting room available for suppliers and drivers and so on. You'll be catered for too, obviously…' He smiled. 'It'll likely be a version of the wedding breakfast, so pretty decent.'

'Sounds good.'

And then his smile faded a little. 'Thanks again for helping me out with the garb.'

There it was, that look behind the look again… messing with her senses, her imagination.

She turned away to cut free. 'You're wel-come…'

And then her heart stopped dead.

Jamie! Booted and suited. Opening the rear door of his beloved luxury sedan for a stunning-looking woman in a fuchsia suit and black heels.

She felt her eyes staring, her lungs slowly crimping. Jamie… Here… Right where she was. *Oh, God!* And if he was here, she couldn't be. Not after all the pain she'd caused him. She'd only see it in his eyes again—the hurt, maybe loathing, or maybe some little gloating joy because she'd failed. Not that he'd ever been that kind of man, but she might have turned him into one, mightn't she? Ruined him for love…for trust.

Whatever!

She couldn't bear it. Couldn't be—

'Tommie, are you okay?' Max was peering at her, concern etched on his face. 'You look like you've seen a ghost.'

Her heart lunged. *What to say?* Then again, if she was upfront about it then at least he would get why she wanted to leave, hopefully sanction it.

She drew in a breath and looked at him. 'That's because I sort of have.' She jerked her head in Jamie's direction. 'See that chauffeur over there, with the woman in pink?'

Max's gaze arrowed through the windscreen and back 'Yes, I see him.'

'Well, he's my ex.'

'Your ex?' There was that look again, search-ing, then softening. 'I'm guessing it didn't end well?'

She felt a twist inside. All over his face that he thought Jamie was the one who'd hurt *her*—but she couldn't get into that with him now...not when Jamie was only feet away, might look up at any second and see her.

She swallowed hard. 'No, it didn't. So, if it's all right with you, I'll go into the village or some-thing...wait there. I'm sorry, but I just can't be here if he is.'

'Of course...' Nodding, frowning a bit. 'What-ever you want...' And then he was moving back, reaching for the door. 'Mind, I want to leave straight after Lucy and Fraser have danced their first dance, so be back here for seven-thirty sharp, okay? Right in this spot. Not a second later.'

Her heart squeezed. Because he didn't want to be here either, did he? Both of them, exactly where they didn't want to be.

She smiled to bolster him. 'Seven-thirty sharp. I'll be here. I promise.'

Max reached for the pillar, steadying himself. That last drink had probably been one drink too many. Or maybe it was those last two. *Two too many!* For crying out loud, though, listening to Gerald issuing forth from the next table, giving it his 'man of the people' routine—listening because Gerald's booming voice made it impossible *not* to listen—was enough to drive anyone to drink…make them want to numb their ears!

He straightened, trying to focus on the cars out front. *There!* Tommie was waiting exactly where he'd asked her to wait. He felt a stir in his chest. At least *she* was reliable. At least he could count on *her.* Not like dear cousin Lucy. When he'd hugged her after the ceremony, she'd whispered to him that she'd put him with Fliss and Gavin, on a separate table from Tamsin and Gerald. What she hadn't said was that their two tables were right next to each other!

He looked at the steps, lining himself up to descend.

Or maybe it hadn't been Lucy's doing but Fliss, sticking her oar in at the hen do, saying to Luce that *she* wanted to be close enough to chat to Mum and Dad even if he didn't. Maybe Lucy had simply been trying to compromise, trying to make them all happy *Whatever!* The upshot had been misery. For him, anyway.

He launched himself down the steps, and then somehow the car was gliding up, idling right in front of him. He reached for the rear door handle then pulled his hand away. No… *No, no, no, no, no!* He was sick of riding in the back, of seeing the headrest every time he looked ahead... sick of always having to raise his voice slightly every time he wanted to talk to Tommie. How could two people have a flowing conversation like that?

Enough!

He wasn't a back seat person. Never had been.

He seized the passenger door handle, yanked it open and got in.

'Oh!' Tommie drew back a little. 'You're in the front!'

'Yes, I am.' His heart paused. Was he making her uncomfortable? Too damn fogged to have even considered it. He licked his lips quickly. 'You don't mind, do you?'

She shook her head. 'No, of course not. It's your car. You can sit where you like.'

'I think that was my thinking too...' He pulled at the seatbelt, getting it on the second attempt. 'But I'm sorry if I've shocked you.'

'No need to be sorry...'

Her gaze was taking him in piece by piece, it felt like, as she waited for him to click the belt into place—which he managed on the first attempt, thankfully. And then she was easing the car forward, making the gravel pop.

'Also, I'm not "shocked".' Her eyes glanced over. 'You surprised me, that's all.'

'I don't see how...' He tugged at his tie so he could get to his top shirt button. At least he could *undo* it unaided. 'I'm a driver, Tommie, not a passenger. I hate sitting in the back and that's the truth. I want to look ahead, see the road, see what's coming...' He rolled his head back against the rest. 'I like to know what's coming...'

Such as knowing where he was sitting at the wedding breakfast. If he'd known what was in store, he could have sneaked in ahead and swapped some name cards around, put himself on the kids' table with the crayons and the bubbles and the easy-to-eat food.

He looked at Tommie. 'I like to know the script.'

She smiled. 'I get that about you.' And then her gaze turned ahead. 'So, how was the wedding?'

What to say?

'It was a nice ceremony.'

'What I meant was, how did the hiding thing work out?'

That frankness again.

'Not as well as your hiding thing worked out, I imagine.'

Her features tightened slightly. 'Yes, well, I was in a position to leave—you weren't.' And then, as if she could sense that he was thinking of asking her about it, she swept on. 'So, I'm assuming, if it didn't work out well, that means you were found…?'

He let his eyes close. 'Not so much *found* as hoodwinked.'

'By?'

'My cousin. She put me on a table that was right next to—' His pulse jumped. What was he doing? Blabbing! Too fogged to remember that Tommie didn't know his story—that he couldn't talk about this…that he never talked about this with anyone…hadn't since his therapy days.

'Right next to who?'

She was pursuing it, of course.

'No one.' He forced his eyelids to open, looked over. 'Forget it. It doesn't matter.'

She scrunched her face up. 'Are you sure about that?'

Cryptic look…sliding her eyebrows up. Like Fliss with that whole *Do-you-really-know-your-self?* angle.

'What do you mean?'

She sighed. 'You've been drinking, Max, and I might be wrong, but it seems to me that that's got more to do with this thing you say *"doesn't matter"* than it has with the happy occasion of Lucy's wedding…'

They were coming to the estate road's end now, pulling up at the junction with the main road. Tommie shifted the car into neutral and then she was turning, looking at him.

'I get that you're a private person, and you can tell me it's none of my business if you like, but I can't help wondering what's going on with you…'

Wondering. Which was really just another way of asking him the question. Looking at him with that warm, open gaze of hers, full of concern, kindness, setting those strings tugging. He bit down on his lip. Did he really want to get into all this with her, though? Churn up all the chaff? Then again, it was already churning away inside him, wasn't it? Courtesy of today. And it wouldn't stop until he was miles away from this place—until he'd shoved it all back into its box again. So what difference would it make, talking about it? Other than that it might actually feel good to get it off his chest…help him put it back in that box all the quicker.

He looked into her eyes, felt warmth kindling. And it wasn't as if he didn't like talking to Tommie…didn't enjoy hearing her candid take on things. She'd been supportive about his hand, hadn't she? Listened to his fears and frustrations…helped him with his damn shirt earlier. So why not trust her with this? Talk to her about this? *Why not?* Just to kill time on the road… just to release the valve…

He drew in a breath and looked at her. 'What's going on with me is that I don't like my parents, Tommie. I don't like being around them. But I couldn't avoid it today—especially after Lucy put me on that table...'

Holding her gaze. That look behind the look again—just when she'd talked herself round, got her head together, decided that there couldn't be anything real happening between them. Just when she'd resolved to see him as a friend only, care about him as a friend only. And now, this... this deep, stirring look...this moment that was feeling pivotal, somehow.

Whatever it meant, she couldn't let it slide by.

'So, when you say you don't like them, does that mean you don't see them? Don't talk to them?'

His gaze flickered. 'That's right.'

Her heart dipped. So all that stuff online was true. *Unimaginable*... Not a moment to stay in, though. Better to be moving on, moving on and talking.

She checked the road, put the car into 'drive' and pulled out. 'I'm so sorry, Max.'

'Don't be.' Shaking his head. 'It is what it is.'

'But how did it get to *be* like that?'

Silence. And then... 'Fundamental differences, I suppose, right from when I was a kid.'

His eyes glanced over. 'You know who my parents *are*, right?'

'Yes. They're News Global.'

He scoffed. 'Very well put! They are, indeed, *one hundred percent* News Global, and always have been.'

Emphasising the percentage as if… 'You're saying they didn't—'

'Have time for us?' Bitterness in his voice now…sliding along its edge. 'That's exactly what I'm saying. Here's the big scoop on Tamsin and Gerald, Tommie. They were bad parents. Busy all the time. Self-absorbed. No time for anything but work when I was growing up—oh, except for the parties. Every weekend the hordes would descend and fill our very big house—media friends, political cronies—carrying on until the wee small hours.'

His eyes flashed.

'Want to know why I'm obsessive about my privacy? Why I love my home, my own space, a bit of fricking peace? Because I grew up in Bedlam, that's why! Even after Fliss and I started as weekday boarders at school, when all we had were weekends to see them, it carried on—crowded house, no time, lots of excuses. I hated it. *Loathed* it!'

What to say? Then again, it seemed that maybe

he didn't need her to say anything. He seemed to be on a roll of his own, just unspooling.

'I wanted normal parents...wanted not to live in a perpetual madhouse. I wanted some one-on-one time, some attention. Not because I was a brat, but just because I was their kid. I wanted Dad to come to the karting track with me, watch me, see how good I was.'

'And he didn't?'

'Oh, he promised to, but nine times of out ten he'd renege...' He turned away, looking through the passenger window, his voice flat. 'And when he did actually come he'd be on his phone the whole time, so it was like he was only half there.

Her heart crimped. Not like her dad, then... When his shifts had allowed, he'd used to come watch her and Billie at their ballet class, never once dropping his gaze, never once not brimming with pride even though they had four left feet between them. And Gerald Scott hadn't even put his phone down long enough to watch his son doing the thing he loved. She felt tears welling up from her chest. How must that have made Max feel? Surely even less important than he'd felt already.

So much for a so-called privilege.

So much for the silver spoon!

She swallowed hard. 'So, you hold it against them?'

'Too right I do. But I haven't got to the kicker yet. After all the time they didn't give me growing up, fast forward a few years and they're up in arms because I'm not falling over myself to join News Global, like Fliss did.'

Fliss... What was her take on things?

She checked the road behind them, then glanced over. 'So Fliss was okay with it all? Didn't mind the way things were when you were growing up?'

'Oh, she'd get hacked off sometimes on my account, because I was her little brother and she knew it was hard for me, but she was all right with it herself.' He sighed. 'She's more like them than I am. She used to like all the craziness... listening to the heated political debates—especially as she got older. She was always going to join NG.'

'But you wanted to tick them off, so you didn't?'

Another scoff. 'I think a jury would pardon me if I'd set off with that intention, but it wasn't like that. I trained as a journalist, after all, following the family tradition. I just didn't have it in me to do the nepotistic thing—jump straight into a plum job at NG. I wanted to earn my stripes honestly, you know. So I went to Focus News instead...moved through the various departments until I landed up on the showbiz desk.

And it was like...*bazinga!* It felt right. I was good at it. Good at getting celebs to trust me... good at getting exclusives. I didn't want to move on. I came into my own, I suppose, found my spotlight...'

A spotlight he'd never found at home...

He was rubbing his injured fingers now, talking on, more relaxed suddenly.

'The rest was circumstantial. I got to know a lot of showbiz people, had a lot of contacts. It was a no-brainer to move into celebrity PR... run my own show. Gerald and Tamsin took the huff, of course, called it "trite" and "pointless", went on and on at me about what a disappointment I was to them because I wasn't a hard-hitting political journalist at News Global. That's when I bowed out...called time on the whole filial relationship.'

He let out a sad-sounding sigh.

'There's only so much a soul can take, you know, and I'd had enough. I did some therapy, got some perspective on Tamsin and Gerald— and on myself.' His gaze flickered over, attached to a pale smile. 'I've got it under control now. I love what I do—love looking after my celebs and misfits. And, not to be crass about it, I've made a lot of money out of it...built my own castle. If Tamsin and Gerald can't compute, can't see any merit in it, then that's their problem, not mine.'

Her heart dipped for him. 'Except that being around them drives you to drink...'

He chortled. 'Oh, don't read too much into that. I was just trying to numb my ears because Gerald's very loud voice was spouting the usual rubbish and I couldn't remove myself. You know, the man actually *believes* he's a socialist! Ask him the name of his own cleaner, I say, then you'll find out how much a "man of the people" Gerald Scott is... Because I guarantee you, Tommie, he wouldn't have a clue.'

Whereas Max *did* know the names of all his people, didn't he? And everyone else's. He greeted hotel doormen by name...all the staff. Everywhere they went he knew names, acknowledged people. Her heart pinched. Was it because he'd felt unacknowledged growing up? Didn't want to make anyone else feel like that?

She touched the indicator, slowing to turn onto the motorway slip road. So much to take in, and so much more to Max than she'd ever imagined—all of it good. Billie had been right about him all along, hadn't she? Max *was* noble. But he was so much more than that. He was principled, decent, honest and...

Her heart pulsed. Looking across at her with an irresistible smile hanging on his lips.

'Have I achieved the impossible and stunned Tommie Seager into actual silence?'

She felt her own lips curving up. 'No. I'm just taking it in, that's all.'

'Are you shocked?'

'A bit.' She filtered the car into the flow of traffic, then looked over. 'Mostly I'm just glad that you told me.'

His gaze softened. 'I'm glad too...' And then he was looking down, massaging his injured fingers again. 'I don't usually...'

Struggling for words now, but that was fine.

She focused ahead. 'I know you don't—but it's good to talk, right?'

'Yeah.' He nodded, and then suddenly he was looking up again, a new smile on his lips. 'But it's your turn now...' He angled himself towards her. 'Tell me about your family...all the Seager secrets.'

Dancing eyes. Sadly, soon to be disappointed.

'I've already fessed up my only family secret—at the interview.'

'What secret?'

'Great-Aunt Thomasina, of course—my almost namesake.'

'That's your biggest family secret?'

She felt a giggle coming. 'Tragic, isn't it?'

He smiled. 'No, it's actually quite heartening.' And then he was lolling his head back against the rest, fixing her with a slanting downward gaze. 'You've got to give me something, though.

What about if you tell me about your dad, since I told you about Gerald.'

Happy ground!

'Okay, well…my dad's called Ian, and he's a train driver.'

'Seriously?' Staring at her. 'Did he ever take you to work? Did you ever get to sit up front while he was driving?'

She felt warmth reaching up into her chest. He was genuinely excited. He wasn't trying to be cute or pretending to be impressed, this billionaire son of a billionaire, this honey of a man who hadn't taken the express route to a glittering career at News Global, who'd wanted to earn his stripes honestly.

She felt her heart softening, flowing out to him. Dad would like him, for sure. Not as much as she did, though. No one could like Max more than she did at this moment.

'He took us into the cab, yes—but not when he was driving, because it was against the rules. He'd let us sit up on the seat and *pretend* we were driving, though.' She felt a memory loosening, a chuckle coming. 'He pulled a blinder once. I was on the seat, pushing buttons, pretending I was driving, and the train beside us started to move…'

'Which made you think *you* were the one moving…' Max was laughing, already there.

'Exactly! But Dad was like, "What have you

done, Tommie? Don't tell me you touched the red button? Because that's the *Non-stop to Birmingham* button." And I was like, totally panicking, because Dad's looking at me with this worried face he can put on, reeling me in... Because I *had* touched the red button—which he jolly well knew!'

Max chucked softly. 'You adore him, don't you?'

'I do...' She felt unexpected tears welling. She was so lucky to have her dad—a feeling Max had probably never experienced with Gerald.

She swallowed hard. 'He's always been there for me...' Encouraging her to go to New York, siding with her dreams. But no more than Mum—Mum who'd had a dream and followed it. They were both eternally in her camp, believing in her, and it meant the world. She smiled. 'Both Mum and Dad have.'

'So, tell me about your mum.'

Her heart went soft. 'She's Sally. She used to be a classroom assistant, but she always fancied running a little café. Three years ago she went for it—took a lease on a small, local place with a friend. So now she spends her days making tea and bacon rolls.'

'Are you actually *trying* to make me jealous?' Max was staring over, chuckling again. 'A train driver dad *and* a mum who makes bacon rolls!'

Shaking his head. 'Geez, I do love a good bacon roll!'

How were they talking about bacon rolls now…of all things? Such ordinary stuff, making everything feel looser, easier, warmer. Making it feel like they were becoming friends—proper friends. Making a smile rise inside her…

She looked over. 'Define "good" for me, please. Just so I know we're on the same page.'

He laughed. 'Okay. Well, first, it has to be a morning roll—one of those slightly chewy ones, floury on top. Well buttered. Nice bacon, obviously. And it's got to be brown sauce, not ketchup. What about you?'

She felt a warm beat inside. 'Strangely enough, we're one hundred percent compatible in the bacon roll department. Although I would add that I like my bacon very, very crispy.'

'Oh, God, yes…' There was longing in his voice. 'I mean, I'll eat it any which way, but *that's* the ultimate.' And then he was sagging into his seat a little. 'We shouldn't have started talking about this because now I want one.'

'Even after the wedding breakfast?'

'*Especially* after the wedding breakfast, since I barely touched it. I tend to lose my appetite when Dad's issuing forth. I resorted to wine instead— which is why you're breathing in my fumes.' His finger tapped his knee for a moment, and then his gaze was sliding over. 'Look, I know it's been a long day, but I don't suppose you'd consider going back via your mum's café…?'

'No point. They close at five.'

'Oh.'

Disappointed tone. Tugging her heart out. Putting an idea into her head.

Because he could hardly make one for himself, could he? Getting bacon out of a packet was a challenge at the best of times, even with two good hands. And he could do with something to mop up the alcohol. And how bad would she feel if she didn't even offer?

She looked over again. 'Look, if you want, we could stop to buy the stuff and I'll make one for you.'

'Seriously?' Staring at her, smiling. 'You'd do that for me?'

That, and so much more, for some reason. And maybe she'd need to think about that later, but right now making him smile like this, making him this happy, was the only thing in the world she wanted to do.

She nodded. 'Yes, I would.'

'Wow!' He leaned back in his seat. 'I'm sure I don't deserve it, but thank you, Tommie…' And then he was smiling again, looking over. 'Which means *yes*, by the way. I'm totally taking you up on your offer!'

CHAPTER TWELVE

'THIS IS AMAZING, MAX!' Tommie was beaming over, sunglasses glinting, her hair lifting in the breeze. 'I can't believe you're letting me drive this.'

Neither could he. He never let anyone drive his sports cars. But what could he do? The idea had hijacked his brain, as the garage door was rolling up, that if he was going to Thruxton race circuit he ought to be going in something racier than the four-by-four, and that Tommie would get a happy kick out of driving something with real guts for a change.

Not that the second thought should have been a factor, but it was. Somehow... Quite an important one. Probably because ever since Lucy's wedding—ever since all that business with his shirt, and letting his drunken tongue wag on about Tamsin and Gerald, and especially after all that business with the bacon roll... Tommie in his kitchen grilling and buttering, mimicking the way her mum chatted to customers in the café, making him laugh until his sides ached, looking after him, making him feel cared for—he'd felt the desire to give back, to do something nice for her in return so she'd feel the same way… all warm in the heart area, a little bit indulged.

He felt a smile coming. Letting her drive one of his precious babies was just the start—not that she would ever know. Because he wasn't going to tell her, or make anything of it…the car…this whole day… This was all strictly between him and himself.

He let his smile break back at her. 'It needs a good run, that's all…doesn't like being holed up in the garage.' He glanced behind and ahead, to check the road. *Nice and clear.* 'Speaking of which—you could put your foot down a bit.'

She shook her head firmly. 'I'm not breaking the speed limit.'

He squinted at the speedometer. 'I'm not asking you to break it…just get a bit closer to it. The overtaking lane's clear. You could get past this van, have a bit fun in the process…'

'You want me to overtake the van?'

Smiling over, a little bit mischievous.

'Yes! I'm bored with looking at its boring white tailgate!'

'You *really* want me to overtake the van?'

She was giving him the side-eye now, sinking her teeth into her lip.

He felt a tingle, his pulse moving up. Maybe it was because he was looking at her lovely mouth, or maybe it was because she was toying with him, both of which were a bit of a turn-on.

Focus, Max!

'For the hundredth time, yes! If I'm condemned to getting my kicks vicariously then you're "it", since you're the one behind the wheel.'

'Righto.'

She looked ahead, and then suddenly the engine was roaring and they were taking off hard and fast into the overtaking lane, hammering past the van and the next three vehicles, before sliding smoothly back into the centre lane.

And then she looked over, her lips curving like a cat in a post-cream situation. 'Happy now?'

He felt a fresh smile breaking, warmth and admiration surging under his ribs. 'Oh, yes...' *More than she'd ever know.* Just to be riding shotgun beside her, looking at her lovely face, her lovely smile... 'You totally nailed it.'

'I did, didn't I?' She turned her gaze ahead, jutting her chin out. 'I can't have you thinking I don't have it in me.'

His chest tightened a fraction. There was something about her tone, the set of her features. A little edge there...some competitive fire going on, maybe. Or some defensiveness. Some tender spot, anyway… It felt like a *handle-with-care* moment.

He made his voice gentle. 'I would never think that.'

'Good.' She smiled, her face turning back into Tommie's again.

Oh, and why did that make him feel better? That she was herself again. That she was past whatever that little moment had been. Why did it matter the *way* it mattered…in this deep way, in this foxing, discombobulating way?

His heart pulsed. *Oh, God!* What was happening here? It was one thing to be noticing the physical stuff—her smile, the tantalising rise of her breasts in that faded khaki tee she had on—another to be feeling these other confusing things.

His heart pulsed again. And there was a whole day ahead of them now, wasn't there? All planned out. Not for himself, but for *her*, to give back…

Thruxton… Fourth stage of the British Touring Car Championships. Pretty much the last place on earth he wanted to be himself since he couldn't race, couldn't join in, when simply being there was going to put him at risk of being recognised by fans who might ask him questions about his hand which he couldn't, didn't want to answer. But it was the only place he could think of to give her a day out—to thank her for all her kindness—a relaxed, fun day that wouldn't seem like more than it was, or—God forbid—inappropriate. Which of course it wasn't. Absolutely not! Because Tommie was his employee, his driver, nothing more!

He fixed his gaze ahead, heart drumming. It must have all stacked up in his mind at some point.

Touring car racing because it was exciting, his 'thing'—which made it easy to pretend that he wanted to go and watch, even though he couldn't race himself. VIP terrace—a surprise he was holding up his sleeve—because he wanted her to get the best possible view, which he could pretend was because *he* wanted the best possible view. Casual clothes for both of them because it was a casual day, going around together for the same reason, and because Tommie didn't know anything about touring car racing and was bound to have questions he could answer.

But that thing just then—that jut of her chin, that tone—and then that coming back into herself…all of it was making him feel…stirred, curious. More curious than usual. Curious on a different, deeper level than usual. He wanted to know what was behind that little shift in her mood—wanted to ask, tap into that seam, open it right up.

But what hook did he have to grasp at other than this feeling inside himself? It was like when he'd seen her ex…that chauffeur guy. He'd wanted to know about him too, but she'd given him nothing—nothing to pick up and run with. Which made revisiting it impossible—not without coming over as plain nosy, anyway.

So different from their 'Tamsin and Gerald' conversation. When she'd asked *him* what was going on it had felt almost like a continuation, since he'd already alluded to not wanting to go to the wedding because of 'family' stuff when she'd been helping him with his shirt. And then they'd had that little 'hiding' dialogue going on too—and, most particularly, since he'd more or less poured himself into the car blabbing about Lucy hoodwinking him with the table plan… *That* had called for some sort of explanation!

But these feelings…these curiosities springing up with no place to go…were making him feel dizzy, blurry. Out of his depth. Because what were they, actually? What did they mean? That he was getting attached to Tommie in the wrong way? That he was crossing a line?

He hadn't exactly gone back to sitting in the back seat, had he? He was the Robin to her Batman now, and he liked sitting up front, liked talking to her. Not getting into anything deep, but talking all the same, both of them, about music and movies, and about houseplants, of all things—how he managed to keep his alive and thriving when it seemed Tommie's always died. And about the new twinges in his middle finger that Paul had been reservedly positive about. Talking all the time…

He felt a tingle, his heartbeat steadying. Oh, but then maybe *that* was it! Both the problem and the answer. Tommie was his driver, his employee, but she was also a *friend* now too—the person he spent more one-on-one time with than anyone else. His heart pulsed. *Of course!* That was why he was tuning in to these little shifts of her mood, why he wanted to know what lay behind them. Because he was getting to know her better day by day. Because he liked her… *cared* about her.

As. A. Friend.

He looked over, felt warmth flooding into his chest. That face… Almost more familiar to him now than his own. The curve of her cheek, the smooth plane of her forehead, that tiny freckle just below her ear. *Just a friend.* And these swirling feelings…just curiosity about a friend—about the parts of her he didn't know. Natural, surely. Normal, for pity's sake! Nothing to be scared of. And definitely *not* inappropriate!

'Hey…' Catching him staring, blushing a bit. 'What are you so busy thinking about?'

If only she knew… Or maybe it was better she didn't. He pulled in a slow breath. The main thing was he'd thought himself back out of the rabbit hole, could feel his mood lightening, could almost see the sky brightening.

He flicked a glance ahead. 'I was just thinking that we should get past this very boring SUV…'

'Ah!' A slow smile spread into her cheeks and then she was turning her gaze ahead, adjusting her grip on the wheel. 'Okay… Well, you're the boss, so I suppose I'm duty-bound to do what you say…'

CHAPTER THIRTEEN

'YOU DID GOOD, TOMMIE…' Max was standing by the open passenger door, stretching, and then he pushed up his sunglasses and smiled. 'You handled the car beautifully.'

Her heart gave. *So gorgeous!* And so adorable…surprising her with this car this morning…trusting her to drive it. Not only that but trusting her—*encouraging* her—to give it some proper welly. And now he was twinkling at her, looking heavenly in his jeans and faded red tee, his hair ruffling in the breeze, and she was supposed to…what…? *Not* feel this ten-ton truckload of confusion?

No normal day at the office, this! Not from the clothes she was wearing to the plan, which was to watch the racing together. *Together!* As if she wasn't just his driver. And, yes, maybe since Lucy's wedding it had been feeling more and more as if they were actual friends, with Max always sitting in front now, wherever they went, but still… Aside from making him that bacon roll—oh, and doing up his shirt—there had always been that critical separation before. Max going into his office…she to her usual Canary Wharf haunts to sketch and research; in the evenings Max going to his dinners and events, she to wait in a back room or a coffee lounge or something. But now it was just the two of them. No safety barrier. No script. Although she could actually do with one—could do with saying something instead of just standing here, gawping and tingling…

She smiled back. 'Thanks. Although, full disclosure, now that we've arrived, I confess I was terrified of crashing it the whole time.'

'No, you weren't.' He was shaking his head. 'Or if you were, then you shouldn't have been. You were really good—and I *am* actually qualified to judge, by the way, so no arguing.' He let out a soft chuckle. 'I figure you've got a bit of competitive steel inside you, Tommie Seager.'

He could see that in her? Amazing, given that for all her brave talk to Billie, and the endless pep talks she gave herself, she could only catch that fire, that zeal inside herself in rare moments these days.

It had been there in the early days with Chloe, all right—when she'd thought she was on her way. Before that, it must have been there in her Spitalfields Market days, sharing a stall with

Henry, selling the clothes they'd made…upcycled, reconfigured. Henry liked tweed, had created hotchpotch pants, waistcoats, jaunty caps. She'd been into Bohemian glitz: satin, silk, taffeta… That silent gauntlet going down every Saturday, that little flame igniting inside: whose designs would rock the most…who could sell the most…?

'Hey…' Max was looking at her, his expression worried. 'Did I say something wrong?'

Bless his heart…

'No, of course not…'

In fact, maybe he'd actually said the perfect thing—given her the perfect way to come a little bit clean with him about who she was inside. Which was what she wanted to do—had been wanting to do for a while now. Because holding on to it all didn't feel right any more now that they were sort of friends—now that Max had opened up to her about his family and his hand, and about how he kept his plants so green and healthy! But she wasn't opening up in return, was she? Not really. And keeping her inner workings to herself had felt fine at the start—more or less essential on the fashion design front—but it wasn't feeling fine any more. And the thing was, Max of all people wouldn't be fazed that she wanted to be more than a driver, would he? He had multiple strings to his own bow, after all—

PR, motor racing, a motor sports news agency… He'd most likely applaud her for wanting more. And wasn't she desperate to tell him about Chloe Mills? Shuck off that weight? Not that she was quite up to that yet, but this could be a way in, a way to set to the wheels in motion…at least put them on a more even footing.

She drew in a breath. 'It's just what you said about me being competitive. It reminded me that I actually am—used to be, anyway…'

His gaze narrowed slightly. 'Well, they always say, use it or lose it.' And then he was shutting his door, looking over with a soft smile. 'If you want to talk about it, we've got a bit of a walk to the stands.'

Not pushing. Being gentle. No wonder his clients trusted him. She did.

Looking at him, on the other hand, was far too distracting.

She zapped the locks and set off walking. 'You've very kind, Max.'

'No more than you.' He was falling in beside her, pulling his sunglasses back over his eyes. 'I mean, you listened to me banging on about my tragic privileged childhood. If you want to offload to me now, go for it.'

She dropped her own shades. 'It's not really offloading, as such, it's more that I want to enlighten you—about me.'

'Intriguing…' He smiled then chuckled. 'I'm all ears now—ready and waiting to be *enlightened.*'

That smile…that lightness of touch… He was making it easy to be light in turn, easy to begin…

'Okay, well… So, in spite of my recent *outstanding* performance in your sports car, and my previous jobs, it might surprise you to know that I didn't set out to be a professional driver. It's what I do, but it isn't where my heart is.'

'Hold up.' Max stopped walking, pushed up his sunglasses. 'This isn't some roundabout way of telling me you're quitting, is it?'

What?

'No!'

How could he be even thinking that? And looking at her as if she'd just told him she'd run over his cat—not that he had one.

She pushed up her own shades so he could see her eyes, see she was serious. 'I'm not going anywhere.'

'But you want to?'

'Well, yes—'

'But you just said—'

For the love of God!

'Stop, please!'

So much for being a good listener!

She put a hand up to stay him before he interjected again. 'Look, you're getting the wrong end of the stick. I'm not saying I don't want to be working for you. I'm saying that driving wasn't my first career choice.'

Was he getting it now? The agitation in his eyes seemed to be abating at least. Safe to breathe again, to lower her hand.

'Driving's just where I ended up, okay? What I'm doing for now—*happily*, FYI...' Just in case he was thinking of jumping at shadows again. 'But there's an endgame, more to me than driving...'

Her heart wavered. Or was she deluding herself? It was all very well Billie saying that if Chloe had stolen her ideas then her ideas must have been worth stealing, but for all the sketching she'd been doing these past few weeks she hadn't nailed anything definitive yet. Then again, that was the creative life, wasn't it? Constant self-doubt. It came with the territory—like the possibility of crashing being part of motor racing. No glory without risk.

Her heart stood up. And she wanted glory, didn't she? Some full-fat Technicolor glory to put back what the glandular fever had cost her, what getting sidetracked into Jamie's life and business had cost her...what Chloe Mills had stolen from her. Surging up again now, igniting inside her. That vital spark. The other Tommie. The *real* Tommie.

She looked at him. 'I love fashion, Max. I'm passionate about it. And those sketches you saw…' *Just say it, Tommie!* '… I downplayed them…said they were for me because you caught me unawares and I was embarrassed. But they're not for me. The truth is, I'm trying to put a collection together to show some buyers. I want to be a fashion designer. Always have. That's my big dream.'

His mouth opened, then shut again. 'Wow!'

Looking at her, his gaze busy with comings and goings—interest, admiration, fascination—and then suddenly he smiled, costing her a breath.

'Well, if those sketches are anything to go by, I'd say you're halfway there already.'

She felt a surge in her chest…hot, grateful tears welling behind her eyes. 'You think so?'

'Yes!' He was nodding now, his gaze all warm. 'I said so at the time, didn't I? You've got an eye, Tommie, a real talent.'

'Thank you.' She swallowed hard. 'That means a lot.'

'And thank *you* for saying that it does.' And then suddenly, as if he was thinking she might need a moment to gather herself, he was dropping his shades, motioning for her to walk on.

'We should get going if we want to catch the first race—walking and talking, mind, because I want to know more.'

More... Exactly what she wanted to give him, just for the sheer joy of sharing...of letting him in the way he'd let her in.

'Okay.' She smiled, walking on. 'What do you want to know?'

'Well, for one thing, why didn't you study fashion design? I mean, if it's what you've always wanted to do...?'

Her heart pinched. Thank goodness for walking and looking ahead, for the distraction of the grandstand and all the people on the move, streaming towards the pedestrian tunnel.

'It's because I got glandular fever when I was fifteen—just before my mock exams.'

'Geez, I'm sorry...' Max was frowning. 'Someone at my school got that. It was rough; they were off for quite a while...'

At least he knew the score.

'So was I. The whole thing knocked me for a loop. I couldn't seem to make up the ground afterwards...couldn't fit back in. Partly because of friend group stuff that left me feeling pushed out, on top of everything else. The upshot was that I didn't get good enough grades to go to college. And I couldn't face resits. I got it into my head that I wouldn't do any better next time around...that I just wasn't good enough.'

'For goodness' sake, Tommie! And your teachers didn't tell you otherwise? Or your parents?'

Her heart pinched again. 'Only all the time...'

Dad switching off the telly *Come on, Tommie, let's have a chat...'*

Mum, coming in armed with a box of her favourite chocolate eclairs, putting the kettle on. *'Resits wouldn't be that tough, Tom. I mean, you've done the work already; it'd just be revising...'*

She shook herself. 'I didn't listen, though. I was a teenager!'

His sunglasses flashed. 'You were difficult?'

'Not intentionally. I was just really down on school...down on myself, I suppose. Passing my driving test was the gamechanger. It gave me a boost—opened some doors. As soon as I could I got a job delivery driving, and it was great...'

'I remember.' He smiled over. 'It gave you an encyclopaedic knowledge of London, made you a better driver, et cetera.'

Those careful lines she'd fed him during the interview. She felt her lips curving up. 'You were paying attention.'

He laughed. 'I always pay attention, Tommie.'

Her heart skipped. Maybe this wasn't a normal day, but what could be better than this? Walking along in the sunshine with Max, talking to him, letting him in more, letting herself off the leash. As long as she didn't go too far…

'So…' He was looking over again. 'Are you about to tell me you loved delivery driving so much that you put fashion design on ice?'

'No. It was actually the opposite. What I didn't say in the interview was that the *best* thing about delivery driving was the money. Mum and Dad wouldn't take anything off me for living at home, so I had money to buy fabric and trimmings and charity shop clothes. I'd take the clothes apart, mix them up, create quirky one-off dresses and skirts. Then I met this guy, Henry Pugh, at Spitalfields Market. He was doing similar stuff to me, but with tweed. I showed him some of my creations, and next thing he's asking me if I want to share stall space with him. I did that for a couple of years. Delivery driving… Sewing at night… Spitalfields Market at weekends…'

'Collapsing in a heap on Sunday afternoons?'

'Spot on.'

'I'm impressed, Tommie. Seriously. It takes lot of drive to work at something that hard.'

'Maybe so… But it never felt hard because I loved doing it…learning little sewing tricks, going at my own pace, trying things out. It was magic. Creating…seeing how people loved my stuff.'

'So you were selling? Doing okay out of it?'

So many questions!

'I wasn't about to float on Wall Street, or anything, but I did okay. I had a following, sold enough to cover my share of the stall and make a bit extra.'

He nodded, then suddenly stopped walking—which meant she had to stop too. 'So what happened?' He levered up his shades with a finger. 'What took your eye off the ball?'

She felt her insides curling up. That would be Jamie, and everything that went with him. And she didn't want to talk about him…relive it all. But Jamie was the key to Chauffeur Me, and Chauffeur Me was the key to Choe Mills. And, no, she wasn't crossing the Chloe Mills' bridge today, but she had to at least step onto it—*make* herself step onto it for Max's sake, so he'd be primed for the truth when she could get up the nerve to tell it.

'Tommie?'

He was stepping in now, with gentle concern in his eyes. As if she deserved it.

She swallowed hard. 'What happened was I met Jamie—that chauffeur who was there at Lucy's wedding…'

* * *

Pain in her gaze…just like at the wedding. *Why?*
What had happened? He wanted to ask…wanted
to know everything. But maybe she didn't want
to talk about this. For sure, she'd started the
ball rolling—opening up, letting him in—and
he liked it, being taken into her confidence. But
this could be the moment to rein back.

He glanced ahead. The tunnel was coming up
anyway, which was no place for a heart-to-heart.
It was the perfect breathing space, though—one
she could make longer if she wanted to…indefi-
nite, even. Because on the other side were the
pits, the paddock, the cars, the crowds and the
fumes and the noise. Timely distractions if she
wanted to use them. It was up to her, and whatever she decided he'd respect it.

He pulled his shades back down, motioning
for her to walk. 'How about you hold on to that
thought while we go through here?'

Her eyes flashed gratitude. 'Good idea.' And
then she was turning to walk again.

He fell in beside her, both of them slowing because the people in front were going at a plod-
ding pace.

Into the tunnel now. Gloomy because of his
sunglasses. But he wasn't taking them off. He
didn't mind being recognised when he was in
the pits with his team, because the people who

stopped to talk to him there would be motor racing fans, more interested in the car and the engine than in him as an individual, but he didn't want to be recognised here—not with Tommie in tow, not when they were halfway through a thing.

He shot her glance. She was looking ahead. Face closed. Was she thinking about that Jamie guy or about him? His stomach dipped. Hopefully she wasn't replaying the moment when he'd jumped with his two left feet to absolutely the wrong conclusion about why she was telling him that there was more to her than just driving. How had his freaked out, idiot brain converted *that* into an imminent intention to resign? Thank goodness she hadn't made anything of it. But it was a litmus test, wasn't it? For him. For how much he couldn't bear to lose her as his driver now.

His heart pulsed. As a friend...

Not worth dwelling on, though, since she wasn't quitting, and since they were emerging into the sunshine now, heading up the incline. And now the pits were opening out in front of them—all the rows of giant team trucks with their workshops and canopies and mechanics, banners blazing brightly with sponsor logos, speakers blaring out the endless commentator chit-chat, and that smell in the air of fuel and fried onions. And everywhere, people.

Tommie stopped dead. 'Oh, wow!'

His heart filled. Nothing closed about her face now. Now she had it all going on—eyes shining, sweet lips curving into a wide, irresistible smile.

'This is amazing. Look at those huge truck things!'

'Team vehicles.'

'With workshops?'

'You need a workshop. And a team of mechanics.'

Wide eyes came to his. 'Do you have all this stuff?'

He felt a smile breaking. 'Of course. I wouldn't get very far without it.'

She was gazing around again. 'I just never considered the scale of it...what's involved. I mean, look at it all...' She was practically squeaking now. 'Oh—and look! There's the track!'

He looked, felt her excitement throwing switches inside him, making his veins buzz as if it were his first time here too. Suddenly it wasn't even bothering him that he was here to spectate and not race. It was simply good to be here, with her, in the sunshine.

He smiled. 'Yes, indeed. Fastest track in the UK.'

Her gaze swung back, full of teasing light. 'I

think you might have said that already—along with how the circuit follows the line of the old Thruxton airfield perimeter road that used to be here, and how it's "a true driver's track".'

All that history…all the facts he'd spouted out to help fill the time when they'd hit that slow patch of traffic. All credit to her that she hadn't tuned out. He felt a smile coming, loosening in his cheeks. Too irresistible not to run with this, tease her back…

'Okay, then, clever clogs. What's the fastest time recorded on this track?' He slid his eyebrows up. 'Bonus point if you can tell me who the driver was.'

She laughed. 'That's easy! Fifty-seven point six seconds, and the driver was Damon Hill.'

'What was his average speed?'

'One hundred and forty-seven miles per hour.'

'You were paying attention.'

Her eyes lit with palpable glee. 'I always pay attention, Max.'

Using his own line back at him.

Tilting her head over, teasing him.

His heart squeezed. God, she was lovely. But focusing on that was only going tangle him up. Better to keep the banter flying.

He tilted his own head, giving her a look. 'Very droll.'

She grinned. 'What can I say? You bring it out in me.'

As she was bringing it out in *him*: this urge to play—*flirt*. And it was wrong, inappropriate, but he couldn't seem to stop now...couldn't make himself care enough to want to stop.

'Okay, so here's a toughie. What's the exact length of the track?'

Her eyes closed for a long thinking moment, then opened triumphantly. 'Two point four.'

No flies on her! He couldn't hold back a smile. 'I'm officially impressed.'

She laughed. 'You should be—although don't get the idea that I hang on your every word. That hybrid stuff went right over my head. All those rules about hybrid deployment: how much, and when.'

'It's a bit of a tangle, to be fair...'

Like the one he was losing himself in right now, just looking at her, at the way the sun was kissing her face, playing with her hair. What he'd give to be that sun...

'So...' She smiled, then seemed to notice she was holding her sunglasses instead of wearing them. 'What's the plan? Where do we go now?'

He shook himself. Movement. Going. That was the thing—and not to be staring at that mesmerising hollow between her breasts. And, of course, there was the whole business of where they were going…

He felt a smile coming, let it fill his cheeks as she slid her shades on and looked up. 'Oh, I've got a place in mind…somewhere with a decent view.'

Max hunkered forward. 'Rory's still leading…'

She pushed her sunglasses up. 'How can you see?'

Because even though she was leaning over the rail, same as he was, staring hard at that place where the cars always surged into view, she couldn't see anything yet.

He grinned. 'X-ray vision, I guess.' And then his hand touched her arm. 'Look, here they come…'

She felt a rise in her chest. *There!* Now she could see them, swarming like angry bees, sounding like them too, with a sound she could feel in her body, reverberating, pushing a thrill up through her, crushing the living breath out of her. There was Rory Bates! Orange car. Leading. Max's chief rival, apparently, and the one to beat. But there was a new car hanging on his bumper now. Blue. Not the green one that had been tailing him before. And then suddenly—some-how—the blue one was surging forward, right below them, cutting through, taking Rory on the inside, going hard, fast, pulling ahead—only just, but doing it. *Doing it!* Poaching the lead.

'Whoa!' Max rocked back off the rail, shaking his head, his expression incredulous. 'Did you see that?'

As if she could have missed it, from here of all places!

She straightened, aiming a smile into his dark lenses. 'Of course I did. Because of the—' she scratched quotes in the air '—"decent view"! Understatement of the century!'

His cheeks creased. 'Are you going to get over it any time soon?'

She felt warmth rippling inside her. Unlikely. Four races in and she was still nowhere near getting over it. How *could* she get over that moment when he'd led her up here and through the glass doors? VIP viewing terrace, no less. Such a view! Starting grid to the left...the corner called Allard right below. A *'fast fourth gear'* corner, he'd said, that delivered thrills every lap—like the one that had just happened.

Never mind that it had taken her eye off the ball just as she'd been about to get back to telling him about Jamie and Chauffeur Me, about how she'd lost her grip on her fashion dreams. That could wait. At this moment she was here on the VIP terrace at Thruxton with gorgeous Max Scott, and she didn't *want* to get over it, or downplay it, especially when it seemed—*felt*—as if he'd organised it just for her.

She shook her head. 'I've no plans to, no.'

He laughed, looking pleased. 'Well, I'm glad you're getting a buzz out of it.' And then he was turning to rest his forearms on the rail again, looking back up the track. 'Geez, I'll bet Rory's spitting feathers. Cillian deployed hybrid at exactly the right moment, and Rory's got none left. This close to the end, it could cost him the win…'

Hybrid again!

She slotted herself back in beside him. 'How do you know he's got none left?'

'I know how he operates, that's how.'

She felt a dip inside. Did he have a handle on her too? Know how *she* was operating? Could he feel her eyes sliding over the smooth curve of his biceps every time his head was turned? Could he feel the weight of her gaze on his nice forearms? She didn't want to keep looking, torturing herself with impossible thoughts about how those arms would feel around her, but she couldn't help it. Because he was tantalisingly close, radiating delicious heat, smelling clean, irresistibly fresh. Hard enough keeping her senses straight without having to keep her eyes in line too.

Her heart pulsed. And on top of all that here were the cars again. Sound. Fury. Vibrating in her chest. Building and building. Louder. Closer. She could feel her heart rising, drumming in her throat.

Max bent lower. 'Here they come…'

She leaned out, craning to see. *There!* Blue car. Orange. Green. Fencing. Dodging. Vying for the lead. And then, out of nowhere, a mighty weight jolted her from behind, ramming her hard into the rail.

She felt a sharp pain in her ribs, a cry hurtling up her throat and out. 'Ow!'

'Hey!' Max was up in a flash, squaring up to the man who had shoved her. 'What the hell are you doing?'

'I was trying to see—'

'By ploughing into my friend?'

The man's chin lifted. 'It was an accident.' His eyes came to hers briefly then returned to Max. 'I'm sorry, okay?' He gave a dismissive shrug. 'I didn't mean any harm.'

Max shifted stance. 'Maybe so, but you seem to have caused some.' And then he looked over, shades glinting. 'Are you okay, Tommie?'

That would be a resounding *no*—and not because of the shove either, but because of what *Max* was doing. Facing off against this guy for her, not letting it go, waiting for her to give the word—which she must, *now*, before the air got too thick to breathe.

'Yes. I'm fine.' She smiled to seem light. 'It was an accident.'

'You're not hurt?' His jaw tightened visibly. 'Because it sounded to me like you were.'

Spot on—but if she admitted it, what then? Pistols at dawn?

She shook her head. 'I got a fright, that's all.'

He stared at her for a moment, as if he wasn't sure whether to believe her or not, and then he turned back to the man. 'Lucky for you she's okay.'

Seriously? Of all the things to say. What would he do if the guy rallied? Came back at him with, *Or what, big shot?* She scanned the faces of the onlookers. All very well Max being protective, but if some wag got a notion to pull out a phone and film the three of them then he could find himself at the centre of his very own PR disaster.

Not on her account—no way!

'Look, I really *am* fine.' She stepped in close to him, lowering her voice. 'And you *really* need to drop it now. People. Are. Watching.'

His voice came back, low and gritty. 'If you're hurt, and this guy needs a talking-to, then I don't care who's watching.'

Way to melt her heart… But irrelevant! What *was* relevant was that if the guy decided to start talking with his fists, Max was going to be in serious trouble with only one fist to fight back with. This had to end now.

She squeezed his shoulder, making her tone sharp so he'd listen. 'Well, *I* do. So, please, let it go.'

Short pause. Then… 'Okay. If it's what you want.' He exhaled audibly, then turned back to the man. 'Seems we're good.'

'Good…' The man stepped back, clearly relieved in spite of his earlier bullishness. He half lifted a hand. 'Sorry again.' And then he was melting away, disappearing.

She felt her limbs loosening. One problem eliminated! Now there were just the few curious onlookers left. Motor racing fans—which meant Max stood a chance of being recognised. And maybe he was finally waking up to that too, because suddenly he leaned in.

'Come on.'

And then, before she could catch her breath, his arm was going around her shoulders and he was propelling her through the doors, into the hospitality suite and onwards, towards the stairs, talking in her ear.

'I'm so sorry, Tommie. I didn't mean to cause a scene—but, seriously, that guy. What a fricking impertinent jerk!

'Exactly! He's the jerk. So there's no need for *you* to be apologising.'

'But you're missing the end of the race now…'

'That's still because of *him*, not you…'

Not that it was important anyway. Because what race finale in the world could compare to walking with Max like this? The delicious weight of his arm around her shoulders, this gorgeous closeness, the warm, deep smell of him. Such a feeling! She didn't want it to end, let alone be the one to end it, but she had to. Because he was beating himself up and she wasn't having that.

She drew back and faced him, felt his arm falling away. 'Look, you did a good thing, sticking up for me like that…'

He pushed up his shades. 'But I annoyed you too, didn't I?'

What?

'No! Not at all.'

His brow pleated. 'But you *sounded* annoyed.'

'I was trying to make you *listen*, that's all. People were watching us. I thought you might be recognised—which you clearly don't want since you've hardly taken your shades off since we got here.'

His lips set. 'Oh.'

How was he doing this? Tugging her heart out, but at the same time making a smile come?

She looked into his eyes. 'For the record, I thought you were very gallant. In fact, for a moment there, you made me feel like quite the damsel in distress.'

The corner of his mouth ticked up. 'And that's a good thing?'

Feeling cared about? Protected? What wasn't to love about that? Her heart pulsed. But Max wasn't her knight in shining armour, was he? He was her boss. Even if, at this moment, it didn't quite feel like it. But she had to remember it, hold it in her head—who they were, what they were. Because this day was already confusing enough.

She shrugged to seem casual. 'Well, it's not a bad thing.'

'Okay…' His smile broke through for a beat, but then it was fading again. 'I need to know, though, Tom—truthfully now—are you hurt?'

Her heart gave. Shortening her name the way Mum and Dad did, the way Billie did. It felt sweet, affectionate, but she couldn't focus on that, not now, not when he was looking at her like this, with concern in his eyes, and that filament of steel too. And maybe he caught her noticing it, because he went on quickly.

'Don't worry, I'm not thinking of going after the guy or anything. I was just thinking that there are medics here, so if you want someone to check you out, we can do that.'

Her heart gave again. He was still looking

after her, making her pulse skip and flutter, ramping up her confusion.

She shook her head to reset. 'No, I'm fine—honestly. A medic's only going to tell me what I know already: that I've copped a bruise...' Maybe if they got going, walked on again, this weirdness would disappear. She licked her lips, felt a tingle. 'Actually, what I could really do with is a cup of tea.'

His eyebrows flickered. 'Well, that can be arranged.' And then suddenly his whole face brightened with a smile. 'We could grab a bacon roll to go with it, if you like, sit up on a bank somewhere...'

That face. That smile. And a bacon roll, too.

Oh, hell! Maybe this day *was* confusing, and utterly discombobulating, but at the same time what wasn't there to love about it? What wasn't there to smile about? Maybe she needed to stop thinking so much and just take it, enjoy it, moment by moment.

She reached up to pull her shades back down, letting a smile come...unwind all the way. 'I think *that* sounds like a most excellent idea!'

CHAPTER FOURTEEN

'THAT WASN'T BAD…' Tommie was wiping her fingers, reaching for her tea. 'Not bad at all.'

He held in a smile. 'Well, it could hardly miss the mark, could it? Since you told the guy exactly how you wanted it.'

'I didn't *tell* him.' Her eyes lifted, twinkling. 'I made a couple of requests, that's all.'

'Oh, yeah…?'

How could he possibly resist doing an impression of the mesmerising spectacle that had been Tommie, ordering a bacon roll…?

He parked his hands on an imaginary counter, tilting his chin up, trying to smile the way she did. '"Could you butter the roll *right* to the edges, please? Top and bottom. Because I don't like dry bits of roll. And I like very crispy bacon. And when I say *very* I mean—"' he batted his eyelashes, because even though she hadn't done that, she might as well have done '"—*very*. And, please, if you don't mind, I'll do the brown sauce myself. Because I don't want too much, but equally I don't want not enough.'"

She let out a satisfying chuckle. 'Very funny—although your mockney accent could do with some work.' And then she was pushing her hair back, smiling into his eyes. 'I was very polite, though, wasn't I?'

'You were. Although—heads up—you had the guy eating out of your hand anyway…'

His heart clopped. As he was. Right now. Eating out of her hand, drinking her in, losing himself in the sweet sight of her.

Not good!

He picked up his cup to cut himself loose, break her spell. No good getting lost, no good losing control. See what had almost happened on that terrace? Coming *this* close to decking that oaf! And maybe the jerk hadn't meant any harm—maybe he really *had* bumped into Tommie accidentally—but he wouldn't know, would he? Too busy losing his rag at red mist central!

He took a long, slow sip of tea. What was happening to him? He wasn't aggressive. Wasn't a fighter. For crying out loud, he was known for being cool and calm in a crisis, for being *in control*. But up there, God help him, even though he'd never hit anyone in his life, he'd wanted to—no matter who was watching. Because that guy had hurt Tommie, ruined the end of the race for her, and he hadn't looked nearly sorry enough!

He sipped again, shooting her a quick look. She was watching the Minis now, on their warm-up lap. Face rapt. Eyes following. Lips slightly parted. *So lovely.*

His heart squeezed. Was that why she cut so deep with him? Brought out this protectiveness in him? Or was it the loveliness inside her—that warmth, that kindness, that honesty—that had him fighting for her honour?

He felt a smile starting. Or was it that she was funny…made him laugh, feel light inside?

He looked again, letting his gaze linger. Probably it was all of those things. Everything she was, inside and out. A good driver. A good person. A good friend… A friend with dreams in her heart. A friend who had been thwarted by glandular fever, knocked back. A friend with talent, fire in her belly. A friend worth fighting for, sticking up for—

Her gaze flickered suddenly, finding his. 'All right?'

His heart lurched. A friend who was also gorgeous and got his motor running every time she looked at him. A friend he wanted to slow kiss. A friend he wanted to touch, undress, feel against his body, skin to skin.

Could she see it in his eyes? Sense it? Had she

felt it, sensed it in him, when she was helping him with his shirt? Had she felt it back there, when he'd put his arm around her shoulders? Felt how much he liked being that close to her, feeling her warmth beating into his skin, her soft perfume filling his lungs. Had she felt… sensed…how desperately he didn't want that moment to end? And if she'd sensed all that, what did she feel about it? What did she think, feel, about him?

He shook himself. As if it even mattered. It was just a stupid fantasy. Impossible! Where was this even coming from? Outer space? Because these were definitely alien thoughts.

Meanwhile, she was still looking over, waiting for him to reply.

He smiled. 'I'm great, thanks. How about you?' He lifted his cup, sipping again. 'Is the tea measuring up? Putting you to rights after your encounter with Oaf Man?'

She laughed. 'It's okay. Not as good as Mum's, but it's hitting the spot.'

As she was with him.

Gah!

He had to get himself off this beat. Tommie was attractive—so what? It wasn't news, was it? She'd been every bit as attractive on day one. For pity's sake, it was the first damn thing he'd noticed about her. Nothing was different. She hadn't changed. Look at her. Same eyes, same cheekbones, same sweet lips—

'Max…?'

'Yes.' He blinked. 'Sorry…what?'

'Truthfully, now, are you okay?'

She was frowning, reaching in with that grey-green gaze of hers.

His heart pulsed. Could she see what was running through his head? His heart pulsed again. Then again, how could she? For sure, he'd stood up for her on the terrace, put his arm around her to walk her away, but those things totally stacked up with what had gone down. As for the attraction thing… He'd been coping with it, hiding it, from the start—hadn't he? Just because these thoughts were jumping around inside his head, it didn't mean they were showing on his face. He was a past master at hiding his feelings, after all.

He inhaled slowly. No, this flurry was all in his own head. He was probably just feeling it more today because they were here, in this strange situation. That had to be the difference he was feeling. Sitting here on this bank with her, instead of the two of them sitting strapped into seats. Being out in the real world with her, in the open air, in a non-specifically work situation. And, of course, he was the one who'd told her she should dress casually, so it was his fault she was in those faded jeans that hugged her rear in all the right intoxicating places, and that vee-neck tee that kept leading his eyes astray.

All this was, was a heightened version of normal. It was nothing he couldn't handle…control. He was fine—could say so with his hand on his heart.

He sipped his tea, then looked her square in the eye. 'Yes. I'm a hundred percent.' But out of sheer curiosity he had to know… 'Why do you ask?'

She gave a little shrug. 'I don't know… You seem distracted.' And then she was putting her cup down, hugging her knees to her chest. 'I was just wondering if you're really okay with being here today, given that you're not racing…'

There was that empathy in her. Oh, and that gaze. Turning him over. But if he didn't nip this in the bud right now she might pursue him, and he couldn't risk stumbling into the real reason he'd come today since she was it.

Not a mess he could afford to get himself into!

Better to deflect, put the focus back on her…

He knocked back his tea and parked his cup. 'I'd be lying if I said I wasn't bummed out not to be racing today, but I'm not dwelling on it. I wasn't thinking about that…'

And now, switch…

He met her gaze, feeling his own softening. 'Maybe I looked distracted because I was thinking about you…about what you were telling me earlier about your dream of getting into fashion design…'

Here was something he could help her with if she'd let him, something he *wanted* to help her with, because she deserved a boost, a leg up— not only because she was his friend, but because she was a real talent.

He smiled into her eyes. 'I was thinking that you never finished your story…'

That was what he'd been thinking? All those comings and goings in his eyes had been over her big dream? Then again, this *was* Max. He'd been all ears earlier. Full of questions and kindly admiration. He wouldn't have forgotten that she'd never finished. And she hadn't ei- ther. She *wanted* to get back to it…edge closer to the infernal rock in her chest that was Chloe Mills. Not that she wanted to talk about Jamie any more now than she had earlier, but it was a good that Max had brought it up—because if not now, when? When would she get the oppor- tunity again to be sitting face to face with him, looking into his eyes like this, with nothing be- tween them but grass and air?

His gaze broke suddenly. 'Look, it's okay…' He shifted a little, massaging his injured hand. 'I got the feeling earlier that it was possibly a tricky subject, so if you don't want to talk about it—'

'No. It's fine.' She smiled so he'd believe her. 'I totally meant to get back to it—and I *do* want to talk about it…' Even if it was a tricky, and painful. Because there was never any gain without pain, was there? She pulled in a breath and looked at him. 'So, I was delivery driving, designing clothes, selling them and all that, and then one night in the pub I met Jamie.'

Max's gaze narrowed by an infinitesimal degree.

Perhaps 'met' wasn't conveying it properly…

She licked her lips. 'What I mean is, I met him one night and started going out with him. He was five years older than me—twenty-six—and his family were starting their own chauffeur business…'

Max raised his eyebrows. 'Chauffeur Me, by any chance?'

'Yes.'

'And he asked you to drive for them?'

'Yes. A few months after it got going. He thought having a female driver on board would help the business, and we were together, so…you know. It seemed like a no-brainer. Also it was easier work…more money.'

'But it took you away from fashion design?'

Max looked vaguely annoyed, vaguely protective—like he had at the wedding, when she'd said to him that she couldn't stay because Jamie was there. Drawing the wrong conclusions. And she'd let him draw them because it had suited her purpose. But she was the devil of this piece—not Jamie. She had to own it now, trust Max with it—because he'd trusted her, hadn't he? Filled her in on his whole family dynamic? And, yes, maybe he'd felt a little bit obliged to, because of what he'd said when she was helping him with his shirt, and because of being slightly the worse for wear when he'd got back to the car after the wedding, but it had also felt as if he *wanted* to confide in her. And she *wanted* to confide in him too, let him in.

In any case, it was all context for why she'd jumped ship and gone to work for his client Chloe Mills. All relevant.

She let her knees go, flopping them out to buy a moment, then met his gaze. 'Not immediately, but over time, yes. I got sucked into the business…' She could almost feel some internal valve releasing, thoughts and words clamouring. 'It wasn't just Jamie's business, like I said. It was a family concern. His dad. His brother Simon. And his mum, Myra, did the admin, all the books…'

Mug of tea on the go, office heater sweating it out because Myra felt the cold…

'They were grafters…thick as thieves. But in spite of that—or maybe because of it—there was a lot of drama, a lot of arguments. I tried not to get involved, but it was impossible. Jamie would come in fuming, asking me to talk to his dad about whatever it was, or to have a word with Simon, and I didn't have it in me to refuse. It got so that between the driving and the placating I didn't have much time for creating.'

Max's brows drew in, eyes all stormy. 'And Jamie was all right with that?'

'Jamie was focused on the business, that's all. And I didn't mean it to happen, but I got to be the same. I hated the family rows, but I liked it that I was pivotal in sorting them out—liked it that I was popular with the clients, especially the female celebs. After everything that had happened at school—getting glandular fever, flunking my exams—driving glamorous people around all day made me feel important…special…like I actually counted. And I liked that feeling. Who knows? Maybe I let it go to my head. Whatever! The upshot was I stopped designing, stopped sewing, stopped doing the market with Henry. But it wasn't Jamie's fault.' Her heart pinched. 'It was mine. I was the one who got distracted, sucked in…'

And now here it was, finally… The dark drop… the dragging ache.

'All of it was my fault, Max. Getting involved, getting engaged…'

His eyes widened. 'You were *engaged* to Jamie?'

'Yes.'

'And then he called it off? Dumped you?'

Way to turn to the guilt screw…make her eyes prickle hot. But of course he was bound to assume…

'No. It was *me*. I called it off.'

His gaze checked, then softened, reaching into hers. 'God, I'm so sorry, Tom.' Using that affectionate pet name again. And then he was looking down, massaging his fingers—to give her some space, probably. 'At least you realised it wasn't right *before* you tied the knot.'

'True…'

Her heart twisted. Never mind the *way* she'd realised—the speed of it, the way she'd knocked Jamie for six. Never mind that she still couldn't quite sweat the guilt out.

'You know…' Max looked up suddenly, his gaze a little hesitant, but warm, keen, brightening by the second. 'I've been thinking… I could help you get into fashion. I mean, you've got the talent, and I've got the clout…some really good contacts…'

No! Her heart pulsed. She needed to nip this dangerous bud off right now.

She shook her head, making her voice firm.

'It's very sweet of you, but I don't *want* help. Not from you, not from anyone. I want to make it on my own, get there by myself.' Was he registering, taking it in? She felt a sudden tingle of inspiration and pressed her gaze harder into his. 'It's important to me—like earning your stripes was important to you…'

He nodded slightly. 'I get that, but still… Just hear me out, would you?'

Oh, no.

'The thing is, Tom, I represent someone who I think would be right up your street. She might be good for some advice…a little mentoring, perhaps, maybe even an internship…'

Please, God, no…

'You'll have heard of her, no doubt.' He broke into a generous smile. 'Chloe Mills?'

No, no, no…

She could feel her heart choking, tears springing up, stinging her eyes. Damn him and his kindness! This wasn't the way she'd wanted to tell him. First part, Jamie—all that. Then *later*—not now…not today, of all days, when he'd trusted her with his fancy car, taken her onto the VIP terrace, stood up for her against that guy, bringing all the heroics—on a different day, she'd have got to the Chloe Mills part. Eased him in gently.

But now? Now she was coming apart at the seams. And he was seeing it, leaning forward.

'Tommie? What on earth's the matter?'

Kindness in his gaze, concern, making it worse, making her tears spill over, so what else was left but to say it all, confess, get it over with?

She wiped her eyes, forcing them to meet his. 'What's wrong is that I haven't just heard of her, Max. I know her.'

He drew back sharply, eyes narrowing. 'What?'

He was shocked, of course, but not as shocked as he was going to be...

She swallowed hard. 'I worked for her in New York.'

'You *worked* for her?' Staring at her now, his mouth opening then closing again, as if couldn't find any more words. And then his gaze was clearing, cooling, hardening. 'And you knew— have known all this time—that I represent her?'

'Yes...' Her heart turned over. 'I saw you once at one of Chloe's parties.'

He let out a short, incredulous breath. 'And you didn't think to mention any of this?'

There was pain in his voice, in his eyes. Loud. Pulsing. Pounding her to pieces.

'For Christ's sake, Tommie. I had you down as one of the good guys. I had you down as honest!'

Her blood surged. 'I am!'

'Not from where I'm sitting.' Shaking his head now. 'Nothing about this in your details! Not a peep. Why the hell not? Kind of relevant, isn't it?'

'Yes, but I didn't know that till *you* opened the door! The agency is so cloak and dagger, so discreet, that even Billie—who works there and put me up for this job—didn't know that *you* were the prospective employer.'

His gaze flickered…conceding, maybe. It was a half-beat to breathe anyway, slow herself down.

'I wasn't trying to pull the wool over your eyes. Not in a scheming way. It was just the job paid so well, and Billie thought the money would help me set myself up, because things with Chloe didn't work out—which is a whole other story, and the reason I'm back in London.'

Another flicker, that felt like a release, somehow.

'Billie was only trying to help. She said no one would consider me for a long-term driving gig if they thought I wasn't a committed professional driver. She said we should leave my time in New York out—that it didn't matter, wasn't relevant. But then you opened the door and suddenly it was *very* relevant. But I couldn't say anything. I decided all I could do was try to seem like a good candidate, so that the agency wouldn't look bad for sending me, then leave as soon as possible. because I didn't *want* to be in this position… didn't *want* this weight pressing down on me.'

He looked away momentarily, as if he was replaying something in his mind, and then his eyes snapped back. 'So, if your plan was to leave as soon as possible—if you didn't want this lie weighing on you—why did you take the job?'

Her heart crimped. Would he believe her if she told him? Or just think she was trying to soften him up? *Whatever!* No more lies. Not to him. And especially not to herself.

She drew in a breath. 'I took the job because I liked you.'

His eyebrows lifted by a derisory degree. 'And the money?'

Seriously?

'Of course. That too! It's the whole point of work, isn't it? But I can tell you I'd have passed it up in a heartbeat if you'd been intolerable…'

He scoffed. 'So I take it, then, that I passed muster?'

Sarky! But was that a spark behind his eyes? Something was glowing there anyway…warmer, brighter, softening the air, making it seem all right to breathe, carry on.

'Yes, at the interview anyway. I confess I had a few doubts after that…but here we are. And you shouldn't be offended because any job is two-way traffic.' She levelled her gaze into his, to press the point. 'I mean, you wouldn't have offered *me* the job if I hadn't fitted your brief, would you?'

His gaze turned inwards for a beat. 'No...'

'So it was the same for me. I liked you, and the set-up, and the money. And...'

'And what?'

He was looking at her—listening with his whole body, it seemed. Her heart quivered. Would his silly pride hate this?

She swallowed carefully. 'And... Well, the truth is, I thought I could help you with stuff. *Be* of help, I mean.'

His gaze faltered, and then suddenly it broke and he was Max again—a little subdued, but himself nevertheless. 'Well, you have helped me. And I'm grateful—indebted, really...' Then his brows drew in. 'But about Chloe—'

'Oh, Max...' She felt her heart dipping, rising, spilling over. 'I *wanted* to tell you so much— have wanted to for weeks. But I couldn't think how to. It's why I jumped on that thing you said this morning about me being competitive. I thought it would be a way to open up a conversation about fashion design...thought if I could just start telling you, take you some of the way, then later, when the time was right, I could get to Chloe, tell you everything...'

* * *

Truth in her eyes…brimming, welling. *Undeniable!* It was doing its work, tugging at those strings, realigning every errant pole inside him, every shredded fibre of his being, back to her north.

His heart dipped. But she *had* shredded him, hadn't she? Let him down with this news. Caused him pain. And even though her explanation stacked up, made sense, he could still feel that initial hurt throbbing inside, and it felt exactly the same as it had used to when Gerald let him down—said he'd come and watch him at the karting track and then hadn't because something else cropped up. And that was a warning, wasn't it? *Timely!* That believing in someone too much, trusting them too much, was a risk, came with consequences. Extra consequences where Tommie was concerned. Because for some reason—probably because she was gorgeous—he was susceptible, vulnerable around her. So he needed to be on his guard, stay level, keep some objective distance.

He pulled in a breath. 'How about you tell me everything now.'

'Of course.' She blinked, wiping her face, and then she was looking up again, meeting his gaze. 'I met Chloe a couple of years ago. She booked

Chauffeur Me for London Fashion Week. I was her driver.'

Stacked up...

A smile ghosted over her lips. 'I was thrilled, obviously. Back then she was my favourite designer.'

But not any more, if the clouds in her eyes were anything to go by.

'Anyway...' She tossed her hair back as if to clear her head. 'Chloe was nervous about the show she was putting on, and I thought if I chatted to her it might take her mind off it. So I got going—not fangirling her, or anything, but talking about fashion. And she engaged...chatted back. And I was, like, in seventh heaven, talking fashion with Chloe-fricking-Mills. It was unreal...'

The memory was lighting her up even now. But then she was frowning again.

'It shook me up, Max. Reminded me that fashion was what I loved. What I wanted to do. What I *had* been doing before I got sidetracked. A few hours with her were all it took. I *loved* talking to her, *being* with her, being part of her *whirl*. I loved getting her to her meetings on time when she was running late—which she nearly always was. Loved carrying her bags and samples into the hotel for her; getting her favourite chai latté for her, so it was there waiting when she got in the car...'

Being *Tommie*, in other words. Being her warm, nurturing self—which Chloe would have liked, of course.

She swallowed. 'Anyway, you'll have worked out already that she offered me a job—as her personal assistant.'

He felt the penny dropping. 'So you split with Jamie and went to New York?'

'Yes.' Her eyes filmed over briefly. 'Jamie was devastated, but I couldn't pass up the chance. Chloe said she'd mentor me...help me. She said she'd pull some strings, rush a work visa through for me. I was touching down in New York three weeks later, all set to live the dream...'

Which hadn't worked out in the end.

He made his tone gentle. 'So, what happened?'

Her gaze flickered, then steadied. 'What happened was that Chloe was different in New York to how she'd been in London. Always too busy to talk to me—except to bark out demands. She didn't mentor me, like she'd promised, didn't let me into her design process at all. I spent most of my time running errands...' She bit her lip, clearly wrestling with something, and then met his eye. 'In fact...full disclosure...that party I saw you at... I did more than see you. I bumped your shoulder.'

'What?'

'Chloe was stressing over the canapés, thinking we were running short. She sent me to organise some more with the kitchen. I was running out through the door just as you were coming in with Saskia—'

'Saskia Riva!'

That jolt. A flash of blonde. Fleeting apology. *English accent!* Buried all this time, until this very moment.

He looked at her. 'That was *you*?'

She gave a little shrug. 'Yes.'

And now she was here, sitting with him on the bank at Thruxton.

Unbelievable!

He refocused. 'So what happened with Chloe?'

'Okay…' Little breath. 'Fast forward a year. Chloe was struggling with a collection she was working on. I think her husband was up to no good with some other woman and it was affecting her creativity. I felt for her, in spite of everything, and I wanted to help, to get back a bit of what I'd had with her in London. So one night I hung on after everyone else had left and went in to see her. I talked to her a bit, then I showed her some of my sketches, chatted about my ideas.' Her gaze opened out. 'I'll admit it wasn't completely selfless. I wanted her to see what I could do…show her I was credible…'

He felt a cold weight sinking inside. 'She shot you down, didn't she?'

'No, but she wasn't blown away either. That's the vibe she put out, anyway.' She pressed her lips together and then her gaze hardened. 'But here's the funny thing: she got going on her collection after that, and what she came up with looked remarkably similar to what I'd shown her.'

He lost a breath. 'You're telling me she stole your designs?'

'Stole...used...was inspired by. It's all rather grey.'

His heart missed a beat. It couldn't be true. Not Chloe! She'd always been straight as a die. A little fragile, for sure, but solid, creatively speaking. Then again, her husband *was* playing away. Everyone knew it. And Chloe was crazy about him. If she'd been blocked, desperate, taking that depression medication she'd joked about in the past, mixing it with booze, she just might have been tempted to...

He drew Tommie back into focus, felt his heart missing again. And those eyes weren't welling up for nothing, those beautiful grey-green eyes weren't lying.

He swallowed hard. 'Did you challenge her?'

She nodded. 'Yes—when I plucked up the

courage.' Her mouth twisted. 'I got a one-way ticket home for my trouble.'

He felt himself staring at her, his heart pinching. The unfairness of it! Sacked for trying to help, for trying to hold Chloe to a promise she'd made. All that after putting her dreams aside once already to help Jamie. Yes, to help Jamie, because whatever she said about it being her fault, it had all started with her trying to help, trying to do good.

He gritted his teeth. He was going to give Chloe a piece of his mind. As for Tommie…

How could he not reach for her hand, wrap it in his. 'I'm so sorry she treated you that way.'

'Don't be.' She shook her head. 'It's not your fault. You didn't raise her. You're just her PR guy.'

'That's under review…'

'No, please…' Squeezing his hand, beseeching him with her eyes. 'It's over. I don't want revenge, I don't want you to axe her—not for me.' And then her features were softening. 'I mean, it's not as if I didn't get anything good out of it. Chloe let me down, but she made me remember what I am, who I want to be.' Her gaze lit suddenly, as if by a sunbeam. 'Nothing's going to stop me now. I'm back on track. So, you know… silver linings and all that.'

His heart squeezed. *Tommie*. Always seeing

the good. He looked into her eyes. 'You're something else—you know that?'

Her gaze flickered, then opened out all the way into his. 'Am I forgiven, though?'

His heart caught. 'Oh, Tom…'

Way to slay him…finish him off. And maybe it was inappropriate, risky, every shade of wrong and unwise, but at this moment he couldn't make himself care.

He freed his hand from hers and put it to her cheek, so she'd know he was feeling every word he was saying. 'Yes, you're forgiven. Oh, God, yes. A million times over.'

Tears rose in her eyes. 'That's a lot of times.'

But she was smiling, leaning into his touch, and she wouldn't be doing that if she didn't *like* his touch, would she? Wouldn't be looking at him like this, with this warm glow in her gaze, if she didn't want, didn't feel…

His heart pulsed. 'Oh, Tommie…'

And maybe this was unwise too, but he couldn't stop himself from moving, leaning in all the way, putting his lips to hers, letting them find the place. *Yes…* He felt his eyes closing, his spirit settling. Right here. Just like this. Warmth, softness, moving in sync now. Slow kissing, achingly slow, drawing up delicious heat. Oh, he could feel himself stirring now, rising and falling at the same time. Top lip. Bottom lip. The ache inside. This was exactly how he'd imagined it. Kissing her slow, teasing himself, teasing her, stretching it out. Taking her full mouth now. And she was right there with him, kissing him back, her lips so warm and perfect, moulding to his as if they'd been designed for him.

Yes…

Tongues now, tentative strokes.

Yes… Yes…

He could feel his whole focus arrowing into sensation. Softness. Warmth. The sour-sweet taste of her mouth. The grain of her tongue. He was going blind, spiralling away, could feel desire pumping, running through him like molten lead, making him properly hard, making his heart drum, fit to explode. Kissing had never felt like this before. Nowhere near. Never as tender, never as deep, never as connected.

Like drowning.

Yes…

Sublime drowning.

Yes…

And he wanted more, didn't want it to ever stop.

His heart faltered.

But it must. It must. Because this wasn't the place, was it?

He slid his hand back to her cheek, then broke away softly. 'We need to stop, Tom…'

'Why...?' Her eyes flickered, then opened, all hazy, and then her hands were coming up, taking hold of his face. 'I don't want to stop, Max.'

He felt his heart surging. That face. Those hazy eyes. *So beautiful.* Wanting him back.

He moved in, kissing her quickly. 'I don't want to stop either, but look where we are.'

'So what we do?'

Looking at his eyes, then into them.

His stomach tightened. This would be the moment to put the brakes on. This would be the moment to remember that she was his driver.

His heart caught. Oh, but he didn't want to remember it. Didn't want to do the sensible thing. Because this un-sensible thing they'd got going on—whatever it was—was feeling so good, so right, and he didn't want it to end. He wanted more. All of it. All of her.

His heart pulsed.

And she wanted him too. Oh, God, yes, she did. He'd felt it in her kiss, could see it in her eyes right now. Desire and something else that was giving him tingles. And he wanted to know how it would feel to make love with her, how it would feel to make *connected* love. Because he'd never felt this kind of connection with anyone before. How could he make himself not want to go the whole way now he'd had a sublime taste?

He moved in again, brushing his lips over

hers, feeling that tingle running through him. 'I think we should go home, Tom. Would you please drive us home?'

She let out a little sigh and then her lips curved against his, smiling. 'Yes, I will.'

CHAPTER FIFTEEN

TOMMIE JOLTED AWAKE. Strange ceiling. Strange slate-blue walls. Strange bedroom.

Max's!

She turned her head. No Max, though. Just that odd noise. Muffled. Drilling. Insistent.

Phone!

She sat up quickly, looking around. *There!* On the floor. Her jeans. She swung out of bed to scoop them up, freeing the phone from a back pocket, squinting at the screen.

Billie.

She drew in a breath and swiped right, trying not to sound as if she'd just been leaping about in a strange bedroom. 'Hey.'

'So, what's going on?'

Her heart paused. Billie's tone had something of the tapping foot about it.

'Nothing…' She got back into bed, clawing the duvet up and around herself. 'Why?'

'So that wasn't you in those pictures, kissing a

certain Maxwell Lawler Scott at Thruxton yesterday?'

What?

'What are you talking about? What pictures?'

'I've just sent them. But you don't need to see them to answer the question. Was it you kissing your boss? Or was it some other blonde who looks exactly like you?'

Her stomach lurched. 'Just, hang on will you…'

She swiped at her screen, heart pounding.

She and Max on the terrace, looking towards the finish line… The two of them with the shover guy, looking for all the world as if they were having a friendly conversation… And one…no, two…*no*, three pictures of…

She felt her head trying to swim. A private moment. Invaded. Their precious first kiss. That warm, deep, slow, tender, perfect kiss that had blurred the lines between right and wrong, wise and unwise. That kiss that had landed her in this bed with the most beautiful, loving, giving, passionate man in the world. And now it was out there for the world to see…

Her pulse arced. *Oh, God!* Did Max know about these pictures? And where the hell was he? In the pool? In the gym, doing planks and those one-handed press-ups? In his office, doing business?

'Tommie?'

She swallowed hard. 'I'm here.'

'So…?'

No point denying it.

'Yes. It's me in the pictures.'

'Wow!' Little pause. 'I mean, obviously I *knew* it was you. And I know you and Max have been getting on better and everything, but I didn't realise you were getting on as well as *that*!'

'We haven't been… Not like that. But we talked a lot yesterday, and I ended up telling him about Chloe and about everything that happened in New York. Which was hard, and emotional, but such a relief, and then afterwards the kiss just sort of happened…'

That look in his eyes, then him leaning in, coming closer, making her heart rush and tingle, and then…oh, that sublime first touch of his lips. Warm, like home, feeling so right, so *meant*…

She shook herself. 'I just can't believe that some seedy bloody paparazzo managed to catch us!'

'Oh, Tom…' Billie sighed. 'If it helps, I only recognised you because I know you so well, and know you're working for Max, but I don't think anyone else would. I mean, for one thing, in the kissing ones your face is mostly hidden by Max's hand. And in the one where you're watching the race you've got your shades on. And in the other one it's just your back and your hair.'

Good old Billie, trying to help as always.

'Thanks, but I'm not that bothered about being recognised. It's more the thought that someone was creeping around us like that. It was a special moment.'

Billie drew in an audible breath. 'So, are you guys…? Are you in love with him?'

Her heart stilled. Was she? That wave…crashing in the instant he'd said she was forgiven for keeping Chloe a secret…that look in his eyes and that other look behind it… the emotion in his voice…his hand coming to her cheek… All those simmering feelings inside her…all the tingles… all the tugs and pulls…old ones, new ones… Freeing themselves in that moment, surfacing, taking shape…

And that shape was…

She felt her heart agreeing, tears welling, a smile coming. 'Yes. Yes, I am…' That dear, dear face. Those eyes. That smile. 'He's everything, Billie. Kind, and noble—just like you said. And he's warm and funny and—'

'Sexy…?'

Her stomach dipped. 'Yes, that as well…'

Driving back, leaning over to blow her mind with a kiss at every red light, caressing her nape, sometimes her thigh, sliding his hand all the way up, just short of… Making her body howl for contact, release. Then it had been the two of them barrelling through the door, kissing, touching, shedding clothes all the way up the stairs. Oh, and then the joy of his body, the firm crush and heat of him, that sublime first thrust, both of them ready, greedy, giving in, unravelling, crying out, exploding. Round one…

Round two had been a slow dance, achingly tender. Every kiss, every touch, perfection. Hands and mouths exploring. That deep light in his eyes that looked like love, felt like love, as he moved inside her, that put a sob in her chest, tears in her eyes, then in his.

Round three—under the shower in his wet room. Bodies sliding together, wet hands. Sliding down to take him in her mouth. Then her hands on the wall, his body behind her, water raining down, steam rising. Mind-blowing. Sexy as—

'Are you in his bed right now?'

She glanced down at the snowy expanse of duvet. She could lie—but why? This was Billie, her best friend in the world as well as her sister. And she wasn't ashamed. She *was* in love with Max—had given herself to him in love. And he was in love with her too. For sure, he hadn't said it, but then neither had she. But he'd made love to her like he meant it, and she'd definitely made love to him that way, feeling it inside her.

'I am…yes.'

Billie's breath hitched. 'He isn't *there* with you right now, is he?'

Seriously?

'No! Would I be sitting here talking to you about him if he was?'

She looked at the empty doorway, then at the room, taking in what she'd barely registered last night. Vast windows framing a view of sun-dappled treetops. Pale overstuffed sofa. Long mahogany chest. Acres of bed…acres of snowy linen. Her heart tugged. Too many acres without Max here. Where was he? Disappearing like this didn't seem in keeping with last night…with the way he'd loved her.

'Listen, Billie, I should go. I don't actually know where Max is right now, or if he's seen these pictures, but he definitely needs to know about them.'

'Okay.' Billie's voice dipped. 'Neville's coming through the door now, anyway, so I need to look busy. Catch you later.'

'Bye…'

She lowered her phone, turned it over in her hands. So why wasn't she jumping up now to go and find Max, tell him about the pictures? Why were there suddenly dark thoughts creeping in?

Thoughts like, Max wasn't the love and commitment type, the relationship type. Thoughts like, if Max loved her, why had he disappeared before she'd even woke up? Why wasn't he here to hold her, kiss her, tell her they were a couple now? Why wasn't he here to talk about how things were going to be from now on, how they were going to manage this thing?

Her stomach clenched. Thoughts that hadn't even crossed her mind until now... The living reality of a Max and Tommie universe. Planet Silver Spoon orbiting Planet South London. And her job! Was she still his driver? She didn't want to stop driving him—didn't want to stop being paid for doing it either, because she needed the money to set herself up. And about that... Max had talked about helping her get into fashion, about clout and contacts... Would he pursue that now? And if he did...

She bit her lip. How would it actually feel, being helped by her billionaire lover? Her chest went tight. How would it make her look to the world?

She hugged her knees. Less credible, for sure. Like a little vanity offshoot of Lawler Scott Inc. maybe—not that there really was such a thing, but taking any help at all from Max wouldn't feel as good as making it on her own, would it? On just her own talent, grit and determination, blazing her own trail, having that satisfaction. And even if she did cut her own honest path, would the world always think that Max had had a hand in it somewhere along the line? Would she be seen as a hanger-on, an opportunist?

So much to sort out. And he wasn't here to help her do it, put her mind at ease.

She pulled in a breath. *Enough!* She didn't want to be chasing after him—didn't want to seem pathetic and needy, as if she was begging for little scraps from his table. But there it was—they had things to talk about and she couldn't just sit here twiddling her thumbs. She needed to find the rest of her clothes, then find him... talk to him!

CHAPTER SIXTEEN

'COME ON, MAX. Who is she?' Fliss was trying again, honeying her tone now. 'Don't be so mean. Here I am, pregnant, feeling fat and about a sexy as a double decker bus, and you're kissing some "mystery blonde" at Thruxton. Please share… permit me a little vicarious delight.'

God preserve him from Fliss's vicarious delight! Especially when the walls were closing in around him faster than he could push them back.

First light… Tommie… Lying asleep beside him in the bed he'd never shared with anyone, looking like an angel with her halo of blonde hair and her sweet, peaceful expression. Dreaming of the sublime night they'd just spent, perhaps, the love they'd made. Tender love. Warm. *Connected!*

His heart turned over. Exactly what he'd wanted, wasn't it? To experience real connection, the deep ecstasy of it, the drowning feelings, the never wanting to stop feelings…feelings so powerful that he'd felt his stupid eyes welling, a sob trying to break out of him every time he'd climaxed. Oh, and how peaceful had he felt afterwards? Lying wrapped around her, breathing her in, caressing all her sweet dips and curves, drifting away…

But looking at her first thing, at her lovely face and the soft splay of her hair, he'd felt all that peace shattering, splintering into blind panic. Because he didn't do sharing. Not his bed. His personal space. His life. And definitely, definitely *not* his heart. Because feeling the way he'd felt making love to her—whatever that all-consuming feeling had been, whatever name you gave it—could only end in pain. And he couldn't put himself in that position…make himself that vulnerable.

Not after years of Tamsin and Gerald. Feeling stung by their neglect and then by their disappointment in him. That was what he was in for with Tommie if he got in any deeper, got to need her. One day he'd need her and she wouldn't be there. She'd be too busy, too absorbed in her big dream—a dream that, quite rightfully, after everything she'd been through, she didn't want anything or anyone to get in the way of.

And what about his tics and demons? He was fine if he could control the script, the narrative, but he couldn't with Tommie. Experience had shown him that already. And what was he without control? Susceptible, lost, exposed, all ragged around his edges. And maybe that version of himself wouldn't be good enough for Tommie. Maybe he'd fail her, disappoint her, get in her way like Jamie and Jamie's family had, end up hurting her in the long run…

All of it, churning away inside him—how was he going to manage this situation?—and then he'd heard his phone vibrating in the hallway, where it must have fallen last night.

Fliss. Breaking the good news that, on top of everything else, he and Tommie had been caught on camera by some fricking low-life paparazzo!

He flicked through the images again. Himself and Tommie on the VIP terrace, sunglasses glinting, looking towards the grid. Another shot with the shover, happily suggesting conversation rather than aggression, and mostly featuring Tommie's delectable rear and the blonde tumble of her hair. And then the kicker—proving that the photographer had been stalking them—the kissing pictures. Several long lens shots, deeply intimate—which was why Fliss was on his case.

Max—her locked-down, emotional fortress of a baby brother—had been caught in the wild, demonstrating finally that he was human after all. But if she thought for one second that he was going to give her rope to hang him with, she had another think coming!

He switched his phone from speaker and got up, putting it to his ear, because all this haranguing was too much to take sitting down. 'Look, I've told you already. She's no one. Not important.'

'I'm sorry, Max, I'm not buying it. I mean, at the risk of sounding icky, you look like a romantic movie hero in those pictures. The way you're cupping her cheek… There's a serious vibe going on.'

A vibe and so much more… But he wouldn't yield. *Couldn't!*

He set his jaw. 'There *isn't* a vibe! It was just a stupid kiss, okay? A second's worth. No! Less. A two hundred and fiftieth of a second's worth. It didn't mean anything. The girl was just a casual date.'

'I don't *believe* you.'

Annoying sing-song voice.

His blood pulsed.

'For God's sake, Fliss. This is me you're talking to. You know I don't do relationships!'

She let out a provoking laugh. 'Are you sure? I mean, sorry to point out the obvious, but look at the evidence… You're Mr Total Privacy. You don't *believe* in public displays of affection! You've never been photographed kissing anyone. None of the models you go out with. Not even on the cheek. No one. *Ever!* Yet there you are at Thruxton, with tens of thousands of people around you, kissing a girl like you mean it. Why not just give it up and tell me?'

His heart crimped. Because how could he tell her? If he told her that the girl was Tommie she'd give him the back-seat, front-seat lecture. If he went further, and told her that Tommie was upstairs asleep in his bed right now because of that kiss—because he'd spent the two-hour drive back, which could have been a cooling off period, fondling her neck and her thigh, kissing her at every red light, keeping the flame going not deliberately, but because he couldn't control himself around her, so that by the time they'd got back there had been no way to dowse it except to take things all the way... Well, God knew what she'd say to that. Except that he was an idiot, and cruel to have started something he couldn't finish...

'Who she is, is going to come out anyway, now that those pictures are circulating, Max. Someone's going to recognise her...put it out there. Is that the way you want me to find out?'

At least he was on firm ground here.

He crossed to the window, running his eyes over the garden. 'Nothing's going to "come out", Fliss. I'm of *minor* interest to *some* motor racing fans and of absolutely no interest to anyone else. As for the "mystery blonde"—no one's going to recognise her from those pictures.' His heart tugged. 'My hand's obscuring most of her face. Besides, she's a total unknown. There are no leads on her to follow, and I'm certainly keeping it that way...'

Except that this was Fliss, his friend in need, his ally, his sister. He ought to give her something, at least soften his voice a bit, and his demeanour, so he didn't seem so over-reactive. If nothing else, it would lend credibility to the lies he was telling, maybe stall her, at least for the moment.

'Look, I'm not being mean. It's just that there really *is* nothing to all this—no story to tell.'

Fliss scoffed. 'That's the story you're sticking to?'

'Yes.' His heart twisted. 'Because it's the truth.'

The truth! No story to tell!

Tommie felt her knees trying to give, her heart trying to crack. How could Max be saying these things? Saying them so matter-of-factly? She screwed her eyes shut, bearing down, but it was too much hurt to hold in, too much devastation, too much rage. To think she'd come to find him to talk to him about the two of them. The future. To think she'd actually thought there could be one.

She pushed away from the wall and stepped into the room. 'So, I'm "no one" am I, Max? "Not important"? A "casual date"?'

He spun round, as well he might, his face blanching, phone hand dropping to his side. 'Tom!'

'Don't you *dare* call me that!'

Tears stung her eyes. Yesterday he'd used the little pet name. Sweet then. Charming. Not now.

'Tommie… I…' He was shaking his head, blinking. 'You've seen the pictures? I…'

Gasping like a bloody fish. Of course he was, caught dissing her six ways to Sunday. But it was fine. She had plenty to say.

'Yes, I've seen them.' She folded her arms to quell the trembling inside, jerking her head towards the phone in his hand. 'I suggest you actually end that call before your sister finds out who I am. You can tell her you've got to go. Got a little *meaningless* business to attend to.'

Shaking his head. 'Don't…' And then he was lifting his phone into view, cancelling the call with an obvious press of his thumb, his face grey. 'I'm so, so sorry.'

Her body flashed hot. 'What for? For kissing me? Having *sex* with me…?'

That hit the mark. Flinching all along his jaw. Good to know she could inflict a bit of pain—if that was actually what it was.

'Or are you just sorry you got found out? Were overheard?'

Another flinch, then a step towards her, a placating hand. 'You're angry... I get it.'

'Well, that's something, at least!'

His shoulders sagged. 'Please, Tommie...' His gaze was wet now, glistening, pleading. 'What I said to Fliss...' Another step. 'It's...' He gave a little shrug. 'I have to be careful...'

'Why?'

His eyes flashed. 'Because she's got this notion in her head that my lifestyle isn't normal—that's why! That I'm missing out by not being with someone. She's aways going on at me to settle down...do the happy families thing like she is. If I'd told her one single thing about you she'd have jumped on it...made a great big fricking thing out of it!'

Her heart plummeted. 'And it isn't "a great big fricking thing" to you?'

Silence. He was looking at her. Just standing there. Looking. Staring.

She felt her head trying to swim, her knees trying to give. 'Yesterday you told me I was "something else". Yesterday you kissed me like it mattered. Last night...' Her heart tore. She couldn't let herself think about that... She swallowed hard. 'And today you're telling your sister that our kiss was nothing, that you don't *do* relationships, and you're telling me that you said that stuff to her so she wouldn't make too much of us, but what I'm not getting from all of this is what *you* think, Max…'

His mouth opened, then closed again.

Which was maybe the answer. But why? How to understand…to even begin to? Oh, and how to stop these tears from prickling, scalding her eyes? How to stop this ache from tearing through her, this frustration from burning a hole in her chest.

'For crying out loud, Max, say something! I just want the truth. What was last night to you? A meaningless roll in the hay? Because it didn't feel like that for me. And maybe I was reading you wrong, but I just…'

How to stand this pain…stay standing upright?

She wiped her eyes. 'I just need to know.'

His throat rolled and then he was breaking her gaze, looking down. 'It wasn't meaningless, Tommie.'

But he wasn't looking at her, was he? And he wasn't coming forward. Wasn't taking her in his arms, kissing her, soothing her, saying it was going to be all right.

One last stupid question to ask…

'So what *is* the story, Max?'

His chest rose on a breath and then he was looking up again, his gaze level. 'The story is that you're my driver. I shouldn't have kissed you…shouldn't have…' He ran a tongue over his lip. 'I crossed a line I shouldn't have. and I'm truly, deeply sorry. It was a mistake.'

She felt her heart cracking from side to side, fresh hot tears welling, spilling. A mistake! He was writing off last night—all the love they'd made, shared, all that sublime, joyful connection—as a bloody *mistake*!

His hand came up, reaching out. 'We can put it behind us…'

Her pulse jumped. 'Seriously?' She swiped at her eyes. 'You actually think I can go on working for you now? After this?' *Unbelievable!* 'What planet do you think you're living on, Max?'

His mouth opened, but whatever he was going to say next she didn't want to know—couldn't bear to hear.

She held up her palm to stay him, forcing her legs to move before they buckled out from under her. 'Not another word, Max. I'm going to grab my things now and then I'm leaving. Don't bother coming to see me off.'

CHAPTER SEVENTEEN

Three days later...

'OH, I'M SORRY, MAX.' Jenny stopped, half in, half out, her cleaning bucket dangling in her hand. 'I didn't realise you were in here.'

No reason why she should have. He wasn't in the habit of loitering in the guest annexe like an aimless cloud, was he? The thing to remember was that he didn't have to explain himself.

He smiled. 'It's fine.' He nodded to the bucket. 'Don't bother cleaning in here for now, okay?'

Her features drew in. 'When you say, "for now", you mean—?'

'Until I instruct you otherwise.'

She nodded, flicking a bewildered glance around the room. 'Okay…' And then she was reversing out, closing the door behind her. She probably thought he was mad.

He turned, heading into the bedroom. Maybe he was—or well on the way to being so anyway. Haunting the annexe like this, clinging to remnants...

He sank down onto the bed, pulling out the pillow that smelt the most of Tommie and wrapping his arms around it, pushing his face into it to breathe her in.

What to do? How to come back from this? How to stop this hard, relentless ache inside him? How to stop missing her, feeling lonely without her? He'd felt a lot of things in his life, but never lonely. He liked solitude, peace and quiet, liked his own company. But he was miserable company for himself now...couldn't stop replaying that awful scene...

Tommie's stricken face. Her beautiful eyes hurt, angry, uncomprehending. And he'd just stood there like a robot, struggling to think of a single damn thing to say—a single thing to say that would make sense to her, that wouldn't tie him in impossible knots. Because he hadn't had time to think anything through, had he? To prepare a response, get a script together.

One minute he'd been waking up, feeling the panic rushing in. The next he'd had Fliss on the phone about the paparazzi photos, putting him through the inquisition. And then Tommie had appeared, blindsiding him with her fury and her pain. He'd gone into defence mode, failed her, handled the whole thing appallingly. And now she was gone, and he was sick inside…empty and aching.

But what the hell was he supposed to do about it? He couldn't make amends, rock up at her door without a script, a plan—without something to offer her. Something other than his own stupid self-pity and loneliness. But what else could he offer her? What else was there? Because he was still the same old mess inside…still scared.

He tossed the pillow away and got up, drifting back through to the sitting room. No photos in frames now, no blankets draped, no magazines stacked. He dropped down onto the sofa, rolling his head back. Neville Cutter had called him earlier about a replacement driver, but he didn't want a replacement—didn't want anyone living in this annexe but Tommie.

Oh, God! If only letting her go meant *actually* letting her go. Dispensing with her. Being free of her. But it didn't. She was in his head twenty-four-seven, under his skin and, yes, in his heart too. Somehow. Deep in. Like a thorn… hurting like one, throbbing away day and night. So she might as well still be here, mightn't she? He might as well have just dived in, taken a chance on them, given it a go, for all the inner peace he wasn't achieving. Then at least she'd have still been here, reminding him to do his active assisted exercises, brightening his day with her smile and her teasing… But also kissing him the way she had, holding him, loving him, making him feel alive to his bones, blissfully out of control…

Out. Of. Control.

He felt a tingle. Was that the key? To embrace *not* being in control? Embrace *not* knowing the script? It wasn't much to give her, but if he went to her and fessed up that he was terrified of being in a relationship, of failing, of not being what she needed, terrified of being rejected, hurt, sidelined, told her that that was why he'd let her walk away, would it cut any ice with her? Would she understand? Forgive him? Come back?

He felt his pulse picking up, resolve winding through him. Even if she didn't, at least she'd know the truth of him—the whole naked truth—and she deserved that. He could give her that.

He tilted his head, catching a glimpse of white under the opposite sofa.

Paper?

He dropped to the floor, reaching to get it. Yes. Paper. A sketch, of course. A stunning one-shoulder evening dress with a long, draping cape. Little arrows and annotations written in neat script. *Red crepe, silk/rayon.* And next to the cape a note: *Detachable?* More notes down the side. *Zip length options. Buttons. Lining.*

Trim. All of it meticulous and so utterly, completely Tommie.

He rocked back on his heels. She'd definitely want to have this sketch back in her hands, wouldn't she? He felt a tingle. Which could be the perfect icebreaker... That was if he could track her down.

He got to his feet. But that should be easy enough. Neville Cutter would never disclose Tommie's parents' address to him, which was absolutely as it should be, but Billie worked for Neville's agency, didn't she? No doubt Tommie had painted him black to her sister, but if he could convince Billie that his intentions were one hundred percent honourable she'd surely take pity on him...help him out. As long as she thought that Tommie would *want* to see him, that was...

CHAPTER EIGHTEEN

TOMMIE FOLDED HER arms over her face to block
out the light, the room, to stop her eyes from seeing anything. But she couldn't block out Max…
couldn't stop seeing his shut-down face with all
that emotion banked up behind it, couldn't stop
hearing him saying 'It was a mistake.'

Lying to her.

Because what else could it have been but a lie?

A kiss couldn't lie! The way he'd kissed her,
touched her, held her, loved her… None of it
could have been a lie. What had happened between them hadn't been a mistake. Maybe it
hadn't been wise, because he was her boss, she
his employee. Maybe they should have put the
brakes on, talked about what they were getting
themselves into before they'd got themselves into
it. But a mistake? No. Never. She couldn't make
herself believe it, nor make herself believe that
he did either.

But he hadn't stopped her leaving. And, as
she'd asked, he hadn't come to see her off. He'd

paid the full contract fee into her bank account, though…

She lowered her arms and sat up, staring at the fireplace. How to even feel about that? Billie's take on it was that Max was trying to make amends, making sure she wasn't out of pocket because of his 'indiscretion', and that she deserved the money, should crack on with honing her designs, getting her sample collection together. But it wasn't that simple. For one thing, it felt wrong taking money she hadn't earned, and for another, she could barely even get up off this sofa, never mind get going again with her collection.

She pulled in a breath. Maybe a walk would help. Ah…except she couldn't go anywhere—not until the courier came with her mum's package. She sighed out the breath she'd just pulled in. Why hadn't Mum just had the package delivered to the café, like she always did? Then again, Mum had probably assumed it wouldn't be much of an inconvenience to her, since she'd barely moved off this sofa since she'd got here.

She reached up, tousling her hair, then raking it back into place. *Geez!* She needed to get a grip…pull herself together. She had a life to live, a plan, stuff to get on with. Her heart swung. Oh, but how to do that with all these torn edges inside her? When this thing with Max didn't feel resolved? When he was all she could think about? When she was missing him—his kiss, his body, even though both of those things were so new?

Her heart caught. So unfair. They'd only just been getting started…only—

And there was the doorbell chiming…

The courier!

She got up and went to the door, fiddling with the locks because they were stiff. Just a good old yank and—

'Hello, Tommie.'

Her heart stood still.

Max! Here! How?

She felt her lips trying to move, to frame words, but nothing would come.

And then his hand was lifting, attached to a sheet of paper.

'I brought you this. I found it under one of the sofas in the annexe.' His eyes glanced at it then came back to hers. 'It's a really good sketch, so I thought you'd want it.'

She found a patch of breath. 'You came all this way to—?'

'No…' Shaking his head. 'It's not why I came.' He swallowed. 'I came to ask you if we could please talk? If you'd please let me talk to you, explain…' Blue eyes, reaching in, beseeching her. 'Please, Tommie…'

What to say?

How to even speak when her throat was filling with tears like this? When her heart was skipping with irrational hope and love in spite of everything.

In. Spite. Of. Everything.

'How did you know where I was?'

'Billie gave me the address.'

Which meant he must have convinced Billie. And Mum too. That courier story had clearly been a ruse to keep her here. Because Mum *always* had packages delivered to the café, didn't she? And if Max had convinced them—if they were part of this—then it must mean they trusted him…trusted him with her, and thought she'd want to hear whatever it was he had to say.

Her heart pulsed. And she did—so much.

She looked at him. 'Okay, we can talk.'

Relief ghosted over his features, and tingled through her too…all warm, as if they were already—

She pushed the thought away, stepping aside to make room for him. 'Come in. The sitting room's on the left.'

He brushed past, so close, filling her nostrils with his warm, deep smell, tugging at her senses. She wanted to reach out, pull him closer, but instead she drew in a deep breath and followed him, walking right into the soft full beam of his gaze.

'It's so good to see you...' The soft beam rippled. 'I've missed you...'

He was turning her heart over, drawing tears up from the well in her chest.

'I missed you too.'

He shifted a little on his feet. 'I can't even begin to tell you how sorry I am for what went down the other day...' His gaze flickered. 'I handled it really badly.'

'You did...'

He nodded a little, as if to himself, and then his eyes locked on hers. 'I've been trying to think of a way to explain my behaviour, and then I realised I'd never be able to explain it without giving up this obsession I have...this ingrained habit I have of needing to control my own narrative all the time.'

She felt her brow wrinkling. 'Which means what, exactly?'

He sighed. 'It means I've spent most of my life striving to hide what I'm feeling...who I am inside.' His lips pressed together. 'I've done therapy, Tom, so I know it's a reaction to my parents. I don't let anyone in past a certain point. Not anyone who can hurt me at heart level, make me feel the way *they* made me feel. Sidelined, unworthy, unimportant... I built myself a shell, learned self-reliance. I convinced myself that being alone was the best way to live, because that way I could control what happened to me…' He ran a tongue over his lip. 'And then you came along, and cracked my shell wide open.'

Her heart pulsed. 'I did…?'

'Oh, yes.' He let out a short, wry laugh. 'From the moment you walked through the door I didn't know which box to put you in…how to deal with my feelings around you. So I was rude, distant. I pushed you away for the very reason that I wanted to get close to you. And then I did get closer to you…let you in bit by bit. And with every bit I let you in, I wanted to let you in more. You know why I wanted to go to Thruxton! Because it was the only place I could think of to go with you that wouldn't seem obvious…wouldn't seem like a date. But that's what it was. I wanted to spend time with you, Tom, give you a day out to thank you for all your kindness to me. A day out not in the car, not as boss and driver, but just as us…as people. And then you told me about Chloe, what she'd done, and I felt so…' His eyes flashed. 'So sick for you, so furious with her—and there you were, asking me if you were forgiven, and it tore the heart right out of me. I wanted to show you how *much* you were forgiven, how *much* I care for you, and that's why

I kissed you. That's why I made love to you—
love, Tommie—like I've never felt it before…'

There were tears in his eyes now, making her
own well, and then he was stepping in close,
taking hold of her hand, his gaze deep and full.

'It wasn't meaningless. It was the opposite.
It meant *everything*, Tommie. But when I woke
up it all came crashing down on me…the mag-
nitude of what I was feeling for you. And suddenly I was scared—scared witless. Scared of
the next step—of a relationship, sharing, not
being in control. And before I could even get
my head halfway around that Fliss was on the
phone about the photos, badgering me about you,
saying how into you I looked, how I looked like I
was in love with you. And I kicked back hard—
because it was just making the terror inside me
worse. And then you walked in, upset, angry,
and I couldn't find the words, couldn't explain.
So I let you go. But, see, the thing is, I *can't* let
you go—because I love you, and I want us to try.
But you need to know the truth, so you can de-
cide. You need to know that I want you, but I'm
terrified of what that means. I'm scared I'll hurt
you, or that you'll hurt me. I'm scared of failing
you, of not being what you want. I'm scared of
needing you—'

'Stop, Max, please, draw a breath…'

Because this was crazy! Crazy wonderful, but

crazy all the same. She freed her hand from his, putting both of her hands to his face, loading her gaze with all the love she was feeling inside.

'I don't care how scared you are, or how scared I am, because I love you. And if you love me too, then that's all we need to know. Love will see us through. I believe that from the bottom of my heart.'

'You love me? Really?'

He was looking at her, with that other look behind his eyes, tearing her to pieces.

'How can you ask me that?' She felt her heart surging, love flowing through her and out of her. 'You must know, Max. Must have felt it.' She stroked his face, filling his gaze with hers so he'd know it for sure. 'I love you.' His gaze opened out…all warm, drawing a smile up though her and tears too. 'I. Love. You. Now, are you going to kiss me, or what?'

His face split, turning his handsomeness into a million shards of brilliant light. 'Oh, yes—and *how* I'm going to kiss you, Tommie.'

And then his lips were on hers, soft, and warm, and it felt like two planets colliding, exploding in her heart. Which was to say the best damn feeling in the universe…

EPILOGUE

Six months later...

'AND NOW HERE she is...' The compère's rich voice was building, milking the moment as only those guys could. 'Meet our New Voice in Style winning designer, Tommie Seager!'

And then there she was. *His* Tommie. His beautiful, brilliant, talented, stubborn-as-a-mule Tommie. Exploding from the wings with her models, running down the catwalk, laughing, blushing, looking so damn perfect, so damn happy.

Fliss leaned in, squeezing his hand. 'She looks stunning, Max.'

He felt tears stinging his eyes, his heart surging with love and pride. Of course she did. She was in one of her own designs, of course—the scarlet one-shoulder cape dress that had lived as a sketch beneath a sofa in the annexe once. The jewel in the crown of her collection.

And now she was stepping up to the microphone, her hand shielding her eyes from the lights. His heart skipped. She was looking for him, exactly as she'd said she would. He raised his left hand a little and she saw him, stilled his breath with her answering smile.

'Thank you, everyone.'

Her gaze slid away, moving over the crowd, and then she was stepping back a little in that shy way she had, blushing again, collecting herself. And then she was at the microphone again, smiling.

'I can barely believe that I'm here today, but I can tell you it feels really, really good.'

A *'Wahoo!'* went up from Billie, sitting a few seats further along the row, followed by a ripple of applause.

Tommie chuckled, the infectious, throaty sound of it echoing around the room, and then she was off again. 'It's been a bit of a journey, and I have a few people to thank, so please, bear with me.' Her chin lifted. 'First, thanks to Deeks & Sanders, Fashion Retailer of the Year, for running the New Voice in Style competition, and for giving me such a fabulous team to work with. And thanks, as well, to my gorgeous models—Melissa, Jody, Babette, Himari and Bokamoso—for rocking the life out of my designs on that catwalk just now.'

More applause went up, with a few more whoops from Billie's end of the row.

Tommie let the room settle, then carried on.

'Breaking into fashion as a designer is tough, so getting the chance to pitch a collection to such a forward-thinking and generous retailer was an outstanding opportunity. So again, Deeks & Sanders, I thank you from the bottom of my heart.'

More applause.

She blinked, then smiled again. 'Next, I want to thank my family…' Her eyes travelled to their row, glistening. 'Mum, Dad, Billie…you've always been there for me with your love and support.' Her eyes flicked to his. 'Not everyone is as lucky as I am, so I want you to know I don't take you for granted. Thank you for being you.' Her voice wavered. 'I love you.'

Applause broke out again and she stepped back for a moment, wiping her eyes, and then she was at the microphone again, giving a little chuckle, holding up a tissue.

'I'm going to hang on to this, because I'm going to need it for this next one.' And then her eyes arrowed to his, locking on. 'Max, what can I say? Except that I'm sorry for almost not listening to you about entering this competition…'

He felt happy tears welling again, the memory flying in.

'You should look at this, Tom. Your designs would totally hit the mark for Deeks & Sanders.'

'I'm not entering. You're connected to it.'

'I'm not "connected" to it! I represent Melissa Kane, that's all.'

'But she's the face of the whole thing—the ambassador for the collection. How's it going to look if I enter? And if I did happen to win, everyone would think you pulled strings.'

'I don't see how they'd think that, since Melissa has no say in the judging and I have absolutely no clout or influence whatsoever with D&S.'

'Even so...there's a connection through you. I want to make it on my own, Max.'

'I respect that, but it's completely irrelevant in this instance. If you enter and win, that'd be all down to you and your talent. Nothing to do with me. All I'm doing is flagging up the competition because it's an opportunity. Stop being so infernally stubborn.'

She dabbed at her eyes, then smiled into his. 'You were right, and I was wrong.' She drew in a shaky breath. 'Anyway, I just want to say, in front of all these people, that you're the light of my life, the love of my life...' Her voice dipped low then, thick with emotion. 'I love you so freaking much, Max Scott.'

And didn't he know it? Every second of every day. She was the best risk he'd ever taken. A keeper.

He felt his focus sliding to the neat bulk of the

ring box in his pocket. A moment for later. On the rooftop, with champagne on ice and the glittering London night stretching all around them. All planned.

But for now…

He touched his left hand to his chest, mouthing words back to her, feeling them to the very depths of his soul. *I love you too. With all my heart.*

* * * * *

If you enjoyed this story,
check out these other great reads
from Ella Hayes

Bound by Their Lisbon Legacy
One Night on the French Riviera
Barcelona Fling with a Secret Prince
Their Surprise Safari Reunion

Available now!

Harlequin® Reader Service

Enjoyed your book?

Try the perfect subscription for Romance readers and get more great books like this delivered right to your door.

See why over 10+ million readers have tried Harlequin Reader Service.

Start with a Free Welcome Collection with free books and a gift—valued over $20.

Choose any series in print or ebook. See website for details and order today:

TryReaderService.com/subscriptions